Cirque Erotique

GW00326539

New *X Rated* titles from *X Libris*:

Game of Masks	Roxanne Morgan
Acting It Out	Vanessa Davies
Who Dares Sins	Roxanne Morgan

The *X Libris* series:

The Pleasure Principle	Emma Allan
The Discipline of Pearls	Susan Swann
Arousing Anna	Nina Sheridan
Sleeping Partner	Mariah Greene
Playing the Game	Selina Seymour
Pleasuring Pamela	Nina Sheridan
The Women's Club	Vanessa Davies
Saturnalia	Zara Devereux
Shopping Around	Mariah Greene
Velvet Touch	Zara Devereux
The Gambler	Tallulah Sharpe
Eternal Kiss	Anastasia Dubois
Forbidden Desires	Marina Anderson
Wild Silk	Zara Devereux
Letting Go	Cathy Hunter
Two Women	Emma Allan
Pleasure Bound	Susan Swann
Educating Eleanor	Nina Sheridan
Silken Bonds	Zara Devereux
Fast Learner	Ginnie Bond
Chrysalis	Natalie Blake
Rough Trade	Emma Allan
Liberating Lydia	Nine Sheridan
Lessons in Lust	Emma Allan
Lottery Lovers	Vanessa Davies
Power Games	Alexa Caine
Isle of Desire	Zara Devereux
Overexposed	Ginnie Bond
Perfect Partners	Natalie Blake
Black Stockings	Emma Allan
Legacy of Desire	Marina Anderson

Cirque Erotique

Mikki Leone

LIBRIS

An *X Libris* Book

First published by X Libris in 1997
Reprinted 1999

A CIP catalogue record for this book
is available from the British Library.

ISBN 0 7515 2043 8

Photoset in North Wales by
Derek Doyle & Associates, Mold, Flintshire
Printed and bound in Great Britain by
Clays Ltd, St Ives plc

X Libris
A Division of
Little, Brown and Company (UK)
Brettenham House
Lancaster Place
London WC2E 7EN

Cirque Erotique

Chapter One

AS DUSK QUICKLY gave way to night Danni Appleyard perched herself on the windowsill of her bedroom and gazed with secret pleasure at the view from the picture window. Although she lived in a nondescript part of West London, the vista was so magnificent she could have been watching the sunset anywhere in the world. It was a real shepherd's delight of a sky. Marshmallow clouds, tinted orange, streaked an endless backdrop of red-gold, the horizon marked by a dark crenellated skyline of factories and tower blocks. Further into the distance the glowing crescent of the setting sun hovered for a while before sliding lower and lower to disappear from view.

Night had finally descended.

Danni loved this time of the evening but for her it was still far too early to think of going to bed. Though Tam, her boyfriend, had other ideas. His job was a bloody nuisance, she thought, as she wandered over to the dressing-table and sat down. Working as a sound technician on one of the breakfast television programmes meant he had to be up at four-thirty every morning to get to the studio. For Tam his job was exciting and challenging, but as far as Danni was concerned it was a pain in the neck.

In fact, she mused, as she leaned forward and peered at her round, wide-awake face in the mirror, their whole relationship was starting to get her down. There were all sorts of little things that bugged her about him, particularly those stemming from a chauvinistic attitude that left her feeling as though her place was in the wrong. And, if it wasn't bad enough having to go to bed ridiculously early, she was forced, by the minuscule dimensions of her flat, to listen to his ritual 'bathroom sonata' beforehand . . . every night.

As she gazed into the depths of her jade green eyes and flicked a long tendril of tawny-coloured hair away from her face, she cocked an unwilling ear to Tam's latest 'performance'. First came the loud, off-key singing in the shower, either operatic arias or a selection of Queen's greatest hits – *Mama mia, Mama mia . . . Mama mia let me go . . .!* Then there were the five minutes – and not a moment less – of dutiful teeth-brushing, followed by a stomach-churning series of gargling noises . . . And so it went on until he finally appeared in her shades-of-blue bedroom looking well and truly scrubbed clean, his fair skin all pink and shiny, his perfect teeth positively blinding in their whiteness.

She only hoped to God that tonight he wouldn't come in and start flossing his teeth in front of her or she would throw up.

2

Tam was fanatical about a lot of things but dental hygiene was the worst of them. He was so fastidious that he flatly refused to give *her* the sort of oral attention she craved. He claimed it simply wasn't healthy. Although, she mused wryly as she wiped off her makeup, his distaste for such a practice didn't stop him encouraging her to do it for him.

She smiled at her own reflection, noting how her wide, generous mouth curved at the edges, dimpling the hollows beneath her rounded cheeks. Her eyes held a definite sparkle, she noticed, although goodness only knew why. What is it about me? she asked herself. I've got a boyfriend who is totally devoted to himself, practically no social life, and I'm always flat broke even though I work myself to death.

'What a life,' she said aloud as she stood up and slipped off her bathrobe. 'Twenty-six? I feel more like ninety-six.'

'Talking to yourself again, darling?'

She glanced up as Tam came into the room looking lean, healthy and disgustingly pleased with himself.

'Why not? You never do,' she countered, immediately regretting her words.

Having treated her to a condescending, thin-lipped smile that infuriated her, he dropped to the bedroom floor to do his customary thirty push-ups before retiring for the night.

Sitting down on the edge of the bed she contemplated the movement of his muscles as they bunched and relaxed under his pale, hairless skin.

3

'I could slip under you and make your exercise routine a bit more interesting,' she offered. She deliberately tried to make her tone of voice light and hoped she didn't look as exasperated as she felt.

'Uh? Oh, yeah, in a minute,' he puffed. 'Must just – oof, ah, that's it, all done.' He jumped to his feet and rubbed his hands together in a familiar, self-satisfied gesture that made Danni feel like screaming.

She couldn't help noticing that his dedication to his appearance was paying off despite the irritation it caused her. He was looking a lot more toned these days. His daily exercise routine and regular swimming sessions lent his physique an enviable inverted triangle shape. At about five feet ten with thick, dark blond hair, he came pretty close to her physical ideal. Although at only five three herself she often felt dwarfed by him.

'You should think about doing some exercise,you know, Danni,' he remarked as he wandered over to the bed and pulled back the blue and cream striped duvet. Without looking at her he picked up the clock, wound it and set the alarm. 'Your bum's looking a bit lumpy.'

Danni bit back an instant retort but as she climbed into bed beside him, he reached out and pinched the top of her thigh. 'Is that cellulite?' he continued mercilessly.

Wincing, Danni glanced down and pushed his hand away angrily. 'No it bloody well isn't! Leave me alone.'

'You don't mean that.'

She noticed his voice dropped an octave as the same hand slid over her hip, into the indentation of her waist and up over her flat torso to cup one of her full, rounded breasts.

'No,' she admitted, sighing as she reclined against the pillows, despairing of her own weakness, 'you know I want you.'

She watched the way his hazel eyes darkened and his petulant lips formed a self-satisfied smile as he lay back, clasping his hands behind his head. Leaning over him she kissed him, her tongue forcing its way into the dark wet cavern of his mouth. Her tongue recoiled slightly as it tasted tangy peppermint. Hot and sharp, the flavour of his mouth made her delicate tastebuds zing.

'Bloody hell!' she exclaimed, breaking away from him. 'How much toothpaste have you used tonight? Half a tube? Why can't you taste of beer or cigarettes just for once?'

He looked affronted. 'If you'd rather have a lager lout for a boyfriend—'

'Oh, Tam, come on,' she interrupted, despairing of the notion that he was about to launch into one of his lectures instead of sex.

Realising that actions always spoke louder than words, she didn't bother to continue but instead walked her fingers teasingly across his chest. Hearing his soft sigh of pleasure she began to toy with his left nipple, pinching and tugging at it until it hardened, then rolling the little bullet around and around under the pads of her fingertips.

5

She eased herself further over him, her other hand travelling down, skating the hard flat plane of his stomach, stroking over his hip and down the outside of his thigh. Feeling her own desire mount she ran her palm over the taut mound of his thigh muscle to slide into the warm nest of his groin. Cupping his balls and then sliding her hand higher up to stroke his stirring penis, she simultaneously lowered her head to suck his nipples and lathe his chest with the flat of her tongue. She licked, she nipped at his skin with her teeth, she breathed her warm breath on his damp flesh. Presently she was rewarded by the sound of an anguished groan.

He surprised her by pushing her abruptly away from him and rolling her onto her back in one swift movement. Covering her with his body he ground her breasts beneath his hands, his palms moulding the pliant flesh while his fingertips plucked fervently at her nipples.

Tongues of fire licked at her nipples from the inside, fanning out from the hard, elongated nubs to inflame her whole body. Between her legs she felt wet and hot. She imagined her labia swelling with arousal, opening out to reveal the true extent of her desire. Her clitoris pulsed, an urgent tingling started in her vagina and she felt her juices trickle from her. She gasped, feeling overwhelmed by the surge of passion that gripped her.

It was always the same story with her, moving from feeling nothing, or almost nothing, to full, throbbing, panting lust in a matter of seconds. Tam often called her insatiable. She preferred to think of herself as normal.

'Please,' she moaned, pushing down on the top of his head.

He looked deep into her eyes, the definite shake of his head frustrating her. 'No, you know I don't like that.'

'All right then, touch me,' she gasped, unwilling to let his intransigence mar her desire, 'stroke me down there instead.'

Knowing he knew what she meant and how desperately her body craved such intimacy, she found it all the more frustrating that he didn't comply straight away. Instead he kissed her, his tongue, still sharply minty, darting around inside her mouth.

Feeling desperate, she wrapped her legs tightly around his waist and urged her pelvis up, rubbing her swollen clit shamelessly against his cock which was now rock-hard. Whimpering with desire she allowed her hands to slide over the thin film of perspiration coating his shoulders. His breath was warm and arousing as it stroked her ear while his tongue laid a damp trail down the length of her neck and along her collarbone. Using the index fingers of each hand she followed the bumpy ridge of his spine, smoothing the flesh either side of it until she reached his coccyx. Then she flattened her hands and grasped his buttocks hard, her short rounded fingernails digging into them.

'I want you,' she urged breathlessly, rubbing

herself more ardently against his cock. 'Finger me, fuck me, fill me up.'

Though heavy-lidded, her eyes couldn't fail to notice the flicker of distaste that passed over his face.

'That's not very ladylike,' he mumbled, burying his head in the crook of her neck.

She almost hit him then. 'Sod being ladylike! We're in bed now, remember? We're supposed to be able to express ourselves any way we want to.'

'Well, I don't like you telling me what to do and when to do it.'

Slowly, Danni unwound her legs. All at once she felt her passion for him abate. She pulled his head back up and looked at him with tears of frustration and disappointment glistening in her eyes.

'This just isn't working, is it?' she said in a cracked voice. 'I mean all this, you and me, living together and everything. It just isn't working out the way I'd imagined.'

'Nor for me either,' Tam replied evenly. 'You're always moaning.'

'I am not!' Feeling furious now, Danni struggled out from beneath him and sat up, cross-legged, on the bed. She felt a bubbling anger replace the churning heat of desire that had filled her a moment ago. In some ways, she realised, the two sensations were quite similar.

Glancing down she noticed that her labia were still puffy. The hard bud of her clitoris, all red and swollen, peeped through the darkness of her pubic hair. Ignoring Tam, she reached down tentatively and touched herself there, her fingertips skimming over her desperate flesh. Sliding her fingers down the moist slit between her labia she slipped one finger inside herself. Capturing a small amount of her juices with her fingertip she slicked it over her clitoris, her fingers working to a familiar rhythm. Gradually she felt her desire mount again until her need for satisfaction became urgent, her responses sending a raging heat through her lower body. Her clitoris began to throb and she felt her breath becoming shorter. With her heart hammering behind her ribs she stimulated herself, sliding the delicate little hood of skin back and forth over the tip of her swollen bud.

She didn't look up at Tam but watched with glazed eyes as his fingers covered hers, pressing them harder against her clit, rotating slowly, then faster and faster. When he pushed her back again she didn't bother to protest but uncrossed her legs and spread them wide, bending them at the knees, all the time maintaining the stimulation of her own body under Tam's guidance. She whimpered when she felt a couple of his fingers plunge inside her vagina. It grasped desperately at them, her inner walls delighting to the sensation of his stroking fingertips.

Shamelessly she churned her hips, grinding her lower body against his fingers and her own. She felt wide open and sopping wet, her vagina swallowing his probing fingers, craving more. Dark thoughts invaded her mind, snippets of fantasies . . . being tied up . . . faceless people obscured by shadow watching her and Tam perform for them . . .

She heard herself gasping as her free hand roamed her own breasts, her fingertips pinching and tweaking at the nipples until they became hard and swollen. Her breasts ached with longing as passion clutched at her. For long delicious moments it held her in its grip, squeezing every ounce of lascivious pleasure from her writhing body.

Her climax, when it came moments later, rose and peaked quickly, her internal muscles spasming, gripping Tam's fingers.

'Fuck me now,' she cried, forgetting all about his earlier complaint until the words had already been torn from her throat.

This time, to her relief, he complied straight away and without comment. Kneeling between her widespread thighs he lowered himself until the smooth knob of his glans touched the entrance to her body. His fingers slipped out of her with a soft sucking sound to be replaced by the more satisfying girth of his cock.

As he placed his hands either side of her to take his weight, she wound her legs around his waist again, slamming her body up against his, matching him stroke for stroke. She felt the wiry bush of his pubic hair brush over the sensitive tip of her clitoris, filling her with renewed lust. Gripping Tam's upper arms she arched her back, rubbing herself against him, feeling the warmth of his harsh, rapid breaths on her torso until she felt the first burning waves of a second orgasm.

He continued to move inside her at a more leisurely rate then upped his tempo again. This time she watched as Tam's expression exploded in a look of pure ecstasy. She felt him pump hard, his cock swelling momentarily before erupting inside her. For a few moments he rocked his pelvis back and forth, the continuous movement allowing her to coast on the level wave of a third, far less intense orgasm. Then she felt him come to a gradual halt, resting inside her for a minute or so longer before sliding out of her.

'That was great, darling,' he murmured breathlessly, pulling her into the crook of his arm and nestling her head against his shoulder.

For a little while Danni allowed herself the luxury of basking in satiated bliss, simply listening to the harmonious rhythm of their breathing as it slowed and became even. Then she glanced up at Tam from under her eyelashes, intending to suggest that they start all over again.

With a wry smile she noticed it was too late. Although the clock on the chest of drawers beside him showed it was only a little after ten o'clock, he was already fast asleep.

The next couple of days followed their usual uneventful pattern. Work for Danni meant a half hour Tube ride into central London, followed by eight hours filing, typing and answering customer enquiries at one of the big insurance companies. Then came another Tube ride, only this time at the height of the rush hour, squashed amid a crowd of perspiring bodies while her feet were trampled on.

Tam, who finished work at twelve-thirty, would usually be waiting for her when she got home, although invariably he hadn't got around to tidying the flat or preparing dinner.

Wednesday, though, was different. First of all Danni received a memo from her company's personnel department informing her that she must take two weeks of her holiday entitlement before the end of the following month. Then, when she got home, she found it was deserted. Instead of being confronted by the sight of Tam lolling about on the sofa listening to CDs, she discovered a note propped up against the kettle.

To Danni, it said simply on the plain white envelope. Opening it while she shrugged off her leather jacket, she glanced at the hastily scrawled contents. It was from Tam, of course.

Dear Danni, it read, *hope you are well* . . . She smiled, realising it was the first letter he had ever written to her. *I'm sorry I'm not there but Jake offered me a freelance trip to Hong Kong to do some documentary or other about Chinese rule. Anyway, couldn't turn down a chance like that, could I, so I've taken a bit of leave that was owing to me. I'll be back in about three weeks or so. Don't know when or if I'll be able to call. Take care. Oh, and by the way, the gas and electricity bills just arrived. Be a love and sort them out, would you? Bye for now. Love as always, Tam.*

She reread the letter once more then put it down on the counter. Totally enraged by Tam's thoughtless behaviour – he could at least have called her at work – she picked it up again and carefully tore it into tiny pieces which she flushed down the loo.

Later, when she had calmed down, she sat and thought about what she should do. Tam's unexpected departure had left her in a bit of a quandary. She had hoped he would use some of his holiday entitlement to go somewhere with her.

Picking up a framed black and white photo of her old childhood dog, Rufus, which sat on the little round table beside her, she gazed at it, feeling wistful and more than a little sorry for herself. 'Well this is just great,' she said aloud to the photograph, 'I've got all this time off, no money, nowhere to go and no one to go with. Bloody marvellous – whoopee!'

She sat clutching the photo to her breast until she noticed that the shadows cast across the pale peach sitting-room carpet were lengthening. As she glanced over her shoulder in the direction of the window she realised that it must be getting quite late. With no Tam around she had no one to remind her of the time. All at once she found herself missing his company, which she had taken for granted. Perversely, she even missed the prospect of his night-time ritual.

Sighing, she set the photograph back on the table. 'Suppose I'd better make myself something to eat,' she muttered. Floppy-eared and wearing a dopey expression, Rufus's image gazed mutely back at her. She glared at him, then smiled. 'Fat lot of help you are.'

In the end she settled for a cheese and chutney sandwich, which she took to bed with her along with a couple of magazines she had pinched from the reception area at work. As she munched, she flicked idly through one of the magazines. It seemed full of nothing but advertisements featuring beautiful, smiling people who made her groan with envy. Then, right near the back, she came across a feature about a circus school.

The article stirred a latent interest in her. It took her right back to her childhood, to her eleventh summer when she had played circuses almost every day. Sometimes, she recalled, she had been the ringmaster, striding around in a red tailcoat, wearing a top hat and cracking a long whip – all imaginary of course – or sometimes she had cast herself in the role of a trapeze artist, a lion tamer, or a clown. Most of all, she remembered now with a smile, there were three things she had longed to be able to do: eat fire, juggle and do backflips. How wonderful it would have been to amaze all her friends with her skill and daring. Now, she realised as she felt a familiar excitement stir inside her, the desire to show off was still there. And what better way to boost her self-confidence than to learn these tricks, she mused. If nothing else they would certainly help to get herself noticed at parties.

The image of herself at a lavish society bash – not that she had ever been invited to any – suddenly backflipping across the ballroom, or juggling with the contents of the fruit bowl, made her laugh aloud. I really want to learn how to do something like that, she told herself. However pointless it might seem, even if I never get a chance to show off my skills in public, at least *I'll* know I can do those things.

Despite Tam's absence, or perhaps because of it, she slept really well that night, the magazine left open on the bed as a reminder to do something truly positive with her life for once.

The next morning Danni awoke with a tingle of anticipation without knowing the reason why. Then as she threw back the duvet, knocking the magazine to the floor, she remembered what she planned to do today. Jumping up, she wandered around the bed to where the magazine lay. Pausing for a moment to rub the sleep from her eyes she read the bold type at the bottom of the article. No address was given but there was a name, Fauve Legère, and a telephone number.

'I'll fake a forgotten dental appointment and go into work late,' she told her reflection as she sat down at the dressing-table and began to cleanse her face. 'If I don't get this over and done with, I'll probably let it slip like everything else.'

Procrastination, Tam often told her, should have been her middle name. And she could remember her mother saying time and time again to her, 'I don't mean next week, Danielle, do it now!' Even her boss complained that hers was the only in-tray which had more in it by the end of the week than at the beginning. In return, Danni tried to justify herself through a whole gamut of excuses which

15

sounded lame, even to her own ears.

Her real problem was that she was a daydreamer. There were far more important things to life than reality. Running away with the circus appealed to her sense of adventure like nothing ever had before.

For once she didn't wait until she had showered and dressed before picking up the telephone. 'Do it now,' she urged herself, reaching for the receiver with a trembling hand. 'Ring these people before you lose your bottle.'

She dialled but the phone just rang and rang, increasing Danni's frustration and leading her to wonder if fate really intended for her to do this. Then, just as she was about to give up, it was answered by a woman with a delicately husky voice.

''Allo, Fauve Legère, 'ow can I 'elp you?'

Danni swallowed deeply as she gripped the receiver. 'I'm just ringing up about your circus school. I saw an article in—' She didn't get a chance to finish.

'Ah, I know it. You are interested to learn *l'art du cirque, non?*'

'*Non*, I mean, *oui*, I mean—' Danni broke off. She had exhausted the limits of her schoolgirl French and wasn't at all sure what she was agreeing to anyway.

Fauve's voice was calm and reassuring. 'Do not worry, *ma chérie*, it is my fault for not speaking in English. Tell me,' she continued, ''ave you tried anything like this before?'

16

'No, but I really want to,' Danni said excitedly. 'I've loved the circus since I was a child.'

'Ah, a love of the circus, that is good. That is the first step, no? I tell you, my dear, I 'ave loved the circus since before I talk, or walk. It is – 'ow you say? – in my blood, I think.'

Danni laughed. She liked the sound of this woman and was becoming more determined to join the circus school by the minute.

'How much is it?' she asked hesitantly. 'I mean, er – I might not be able to afford all of the courses. And I only have two weeks.'

'Two weeks from when?' Fauve replied, ignoring her question about the cost.

'Well, I, er, from this Saturday I suppose.'

'That is excellent.' Danni could hear an excitement in Fauve's voice that seemed to match her own. 'It would be perfect. By the end of your stay you would be ready for one of our grand performances.'

'Really?' Danni sat down on the arm of the sofa. She hadn't imagined the course would involve a real live performance . . . in front of other people.

'Yes, really. It is a special thing we like to do.'

'But how much will it cost?' Danni persisted.

To her dismay, Fauve mentioned a sum that was way beyond her means.

'I'm sorry, I've been wasting your time,' Danni said. 'I couldn't possibly afford that much, even a tenth of that would be stretching it.'

She heard Fauve laugh. 'Stretching it – that is a funny English saying, no? Please, my dear girl, do not worry about the money. I never worry about such things.'

Danni thought privately that the only people who never worried about money were the ones who had plenty of it.

'I want you to come,' Fauve continued, 'I like the sound of you. You are young, yes – and pretty?'

Pursing her lips, Danni thought about herself for a moment. 'I'm twenty-six, which I suppose is youngish,' she said, 'and other people tell me I'm pretty, so I suppose—'

'Describe yourself,' Fauve interrupted.

'Oh!' Danni felt taken aback. 'Right, OK. I'm quite short, only five feet three, I've got quite a nice figure—'

'Stop there,' Fauve interrupted again, only more firmly. 'I don't want to 'ear this *quite nice*, I want to know exactly. Tell me, my dear, 'ow does your figure go – out-in-out, or out-out-out?'

Despite her nervousness, Dannie laughed. 'Out-in-out. I haven't measured myself lately but I usually wear a size ten, or occasionally a twelve if the bust is a bit tight.'

'So you have quite large breasts then, yes?'

For some reason she couldn't fathom, Danni found herself blushing. It seemed very odd to be discussing her breasts on the telephone with a woman she hadn't even met.

'They're ... generous,' she said, hedging a bit. 'My boyfriend likes them, at any rate.'

'Your boyfriend?' Fauve sounded surprised. 'He will be coming with you to the school?'

'No,' Danni said. 'He's away for a few weeks. That's why I'm feeling a bit miserable at the moment. I was hoping to go on holiday with him.'

'So you are missing him then – you are very much in love?'

'To be honest, no,' Danni surprised herself by saying. 'I'm starting to think our relationship is a mistake. It's actually quite a relief to be on my own again.'

She heard Fauve mutter, 'Interesting,' and all at once she got the impression that someone else was listening to the conversation.

'So,' Fauve continued, 'you 'ave this delicious figure, yes – and what about the rest of you, your 'air, your eyes?'

Danni stood up and walked over to a tall glass-fronted cupboard which housed her meagre selection of wine glasses and tumblers. She could see her reflection in the glass and so proceeded to give Fauve as detailed a description of herself as she could manage. When she'd finished she heard the other woman mutter something and then her ears picked up a responding voice in the background. A voice that was dark, interesting – and definitely male. Unaccountably, Danni felt her pulse quicken.

'We think,' Fauve said after a few moments had passed, 'that you would be most welcome here. Pay what you can afford. The rest you can, 'ow you say – work off?'

Danni couldn't help noticing the *I* had suddenly changed to *we* but she was too stunned by Fauve's generosity to give it much thought.

Instead, she stammered, 'Are you sure? I mean—'

The answer was firm. 'We're sure.'

While she was still grappling mentally with her unexpected good fortune, she managed to take note of the address that Fauve gave her and promised to turn up by lunchtime on Saturday. Which, she realised as she put down the phone with a sigh of satisfaction, gave her just under two days to shop, pack and generally prepare herself for realising a long cherished dream.

Chapter Two

SUNLIGHT DAPPLED THE bonnet of the red minicab as it wove its way from the station along a series of leafy lanes. Sussex, Danni decided as she gazed out of the passenger window at the passing scenery, was a beautiful county. They had already passed through a couple of tiny, picturesque villages and now they were approaching a third. The thirty-mile-an-hour signs instructed the driver to slow down and told Danni that she had almost reached her destination.

Having felt relaxed during the train journey from London and the fifteen-minute taxi ride, Danni now felt her heartbeat quicken. She felt as though she were heading for the unknown and suddenly remembered that she hadn't let anyone know where she was going.

As she was expecting to return before Tam, she hadn't bothered to leave him a note similar to the one he had left her. But, she realised on reflection, she should have at least phoned her mother, or her best friend Linda. Supposing these circus people turned out to be maniacs, or if she injured herself in some way, who would know of her plight? And if she never returned home at all no one would know where to start looking for her. Unnerved by the possibilities that now occurred to her, she resolved that, at the earliest opportunity, she would walk down to the village and send a post-card to her mother. That way she wouldn't feel stranded. Or, better still, the school probably had a pay phone she could use . . .

'Nearly there, love,' the driver said to her, turn-ing his head for a moment and giving her a friendly smile.

She nodded. She had opted to sit in the front seat and was grateful that the driver of the minicab was genial without being too talkative. Although she had already spent the previous couple of days and the whole of this morning mulling over her telephone conversation with Fauve, she was still glad of the opportunity to be left alone with her thoughts. She felt as though she were preparing herself mentally for something momentous and now, as her suppositions were about to become reality, she found herself filled with an equal mixture of excitement and trepidation.

There had been something about the way the Frenchwoman had spoken to her – the combina-tion of her low, seductive voice and the intimate way she had questioned her – that made Danni's intuition quiver. And the presence of the mysteri-ous third party in Fauve's office, the one who had been listening to her describe her appearance, including the size and shape of her breasts, filled her with uneasy anticipation.

She knew the listener had been a man. As though an invisible thread connected them she had felt his 'vibes' – kind and sensitive yet also darkly, deeply erotic – and her body had automatically thrilled to them. Intuitive and dreamy by nature, Danni felt as though she were about to enter a realm of discovery that involved far more than simply learning a few circus skills. Is this the point in my life where I finally leave my childhood behind? she asked herself, while answering her own question with a certainty, deep inside, that she was poised on the brink of a new self-awareness.

The village they had now entered was every bit as picture-postcard perfect as the others she had seen. Stone cottages, some of them thatched, lined the winding street that led through its centre. There were two pubs, she noticed, and only one grocery shop-cum-Post Office and newsagent. She saw a couple of men and a woman standing outside the shop talking and, further along the street, where it opened out on the left – to what she assumed was the village green – she observed a handful of children playing, while mums with pushchairs sat on wooden benches, toasting bare white arms and legs.

It was late May and extremely warm. The sky was an unbroken canopy of blue and the tarmac-covered road ahead shimmered in a haze of heat. Undecided at first as to what to wear, Danni had finally opted for a pair of loose black cotton trousers and a cream top, which she wore with a pair of black wedge-heeled sandals to make her look a little bit taller. She had brought very little with her in the way of clothing: a few pairs of leggings, half a dozen T-shirts, some underwear, a couple of cotton dresses and one pair of shorts, all of which she had packed into a single holdall. At the station she had bought a couple of paper-back blockbusters, a few bars of chocolate and a couple of bottles of flavoured mineral water – just in case the school was a long walk from the shops. Now, she realised as they drove out of the village and turned right up a steep, narrow lane, she had been right to take such precautions; late-night chocolate binges were one of her many weaknesses.

'The place you want is just up here a-ways,' the driver said as though he could read her thoughts. He pointed. 'See, it's over there.'

Following the direction of his finger, Danni glanced up and to the right. On top of the hill she could make out a cluster of brick farm buildings, behind which she could just see the white canvas top of what looked to be a huge marquee.

'That must be where they put on their performances,' Danni said excitedly. 'Have you ever been to one?' She assumed the driver lived fairly locally. However, he shook his head as he turned off the lane, drove through an open gateway and continued up a rutted track.

'No, it's not for the likes of us. By invitation only apparently. That Madame Legère can get a bit sniffy if folks start poking their noses into her business.'

'Oh dear, really?' Danni didn't really know what to say. She had assumed that circus people were naturally friendly and would make an effort to get on with the locals. Still, she supposed, this was a circus school, rather than a real circus and Fauve *was* French. She laughed to herself then, wondering why she thought it was quite normal for foreigners to be a bit standoffish. 'Perhaps she's just shy,' she offered.

To her surprise the taxi driver gave a spluttering laugh. 'Her – shy? You must be joking. From what I've heard, them in there' – he cocked his head in the direction of the farm which they were just approaching – 'don't know the meaning of the word.' He lowered his voice to a conspiratorial level. 'There are lots of stories flying about these parts and most of them concern some very rum goings-on. Very rum indeed.'

Danni felt her heart start to pound. It was too late to feel afraid, she told herself, and far too late to turn back now. The car was already pulling into a central courtyard.

A couple of dogs, one a large black labrador, the other a white and tan terrier, ran up to the taxi and started barking. As they drew to a halt Danni glanced nervously at the driver.

'Do you think—?' she started to say, but the driver was already opening his door and shooing the dogs away in a loud, firm voice. As he went around to the back of the car to unlock the boot, Danni climbed out of the passenger side. She closed the door and stood with her back pressed against it as the dogs danced excitedly around in front of her.

'Regis, Delilah, come here – at once!' The stern command came from a small dark woman who appeared from around the side of the main farmhouse.

Danni watched as the dogs immediately stopped barking and walked obediently over to their owner, their tongues lolling and eyes rolling in a slavish expression. Despite her nervousness, Danni laughed.

The woman bade the dogs to sit and stay, then walked towards Danni, her hands outstretched.

'Hi there. I am Fauve and you must be Danni,' she said, smiling brightly and gripping Danni's hands between her own.

Danni nodded, then turned to the mini-cab driver as he put her bag on the ground beside her. 'There you go, miss,' he muttered. 'That'll be eight pounds fifty.'

'Oh, right, thanks,' Danni said.

Fumbling a bit, she dug into her shoulder bag for her purse, pulled out a ten-pound note and told him to keep the change. She couldn't help noticing how he cast a wary glance at Fauve before getting back into the car. Flashing Danni a smile, which to her looked falsely bright, he turned the car around and drove out of the courtyard. Raising her hand, Danni watched the rear of the car as, in a cloud of dust and straw, it receded down the track towards the lane. Unaccountably, she felt a sinking feeling, as though she had just waved goodbye to her last contact with reality.

'So, *ma chérie*, you are 'ere at last.' Fauve's voice broke through Danni's thoughts and she turned to look at the petite Frenchwoman, who had a half smile on her face.

She had tried hard to imagine what Fauve must look like and as far as age and colouring went, she saw straight away, her assumptions had been spot-on. However, she had imagined Fauve as a much taller woman and also that she would have long hair. In fact, the older woman's dark brown, almost black, hair was cut in a gamine style that feathered around her exquisite, slightly pointed face and swan-like neck. She was, Danni estimated, some-where around her mid-thirties, although she also had the appearance of someone who was ageless. Her figure was trim without being too thin and she was clad in a flatteringly cut pair of black jeans, worn with a short-sleeved ribbed jumper, also in black, which seemed to mould itself around her small, rounded breasts and fitted snugly against her flat torso and tiny waist. On her feet she wore a pair of flat-soled sandals with braided black leather thongs.

At first Danni found it strange as she experi-enced the unusual sensation of looking down on another woman from a greater height; she was so used to everyone being taller than herself. Then gradually, as Fauve picked up her bag, took her arm and began to lead her towards the farmhouse, chattering all the time about the wonderful weather and so forth, she found herself warming to her hostess.

Although the farmhouse was nothing special to look at from the outside – just a brick oblong with a red tiled roof and white window frames that looked as though they could do with a fresh coat of paint – the interior took her breath away.

The ground floor had obviously been extensively remodelled, Danni noticed. Most of the internal walls and the ceiling above had been demolished to make one vast, sparsely furnished room which seemed limitless in height. The floor was polished wood, the walls simply rough, cream-painted plaster which were dotted here and there with paintings and framed photographs of circus performers. And, as Danni gazed up to the exposed rafters which supported the high sloping ceiling, she found herself reeling with a sensation she could only liken to vertigo.

'Steady on, little one,' a deep voice said in her ear, surprising her almost as much as the strong hands gripping her shoulders.

Feeling dazed, she turned her head slowly and found herself staring into the deepest, most startling pair of blue eyes she had ever seen.

'Ivan, darling, this is Danni. Remember – she called us a couple of days ago?' Fauve smiled over Danni's shoulder at the man who gradually released his hold.

Danni noticed he didn't look at Fauve but watched *her* intently, keeping his hands raised as though poised to catch her again should she falter.

She swallowed deeply, finding his attentiveness reassuring yet also a little disturbing.

'I remember,' he said as he held out his hand and took Danni's holdall from Fauve. 'She of the modest nature and wonderful breasts.'

Danni couldn't help blushing as he spoke, particularly as he cast his eyes appreciatively over her at the same time.

Fauve laughed lightly. 'Ivan, stop it,' she admonished, 'you are embarrassing the poor little thing.'

Fauve's description of her as 'little' struck Danni as amusing. She laughed nervously, glancing from Ivan to Fauve and back to Ivan.

He was, she decided, the most beautiful man she had ever seen. Tall and broad-shouldered, he held himself proudly erect. His tanned face was both strong yet finely chiselled, as though created by a master sculptor, with a straight nose, full, sensual mouth and those eyes ... Oh, dear God, those eyes ...

Danni found herself sinking into them once again and only with the greatest effort managed to tear her gaze away. She had the impression that he was capable of mesmerising her. Not only were his irises as startlingly brilliant as sapphires but his gaze was direct and unblinking, making her feel as though he could see right inside her and thrilling her to the core. The other part of him which she found almost equally amazing was his hair. A shocking white blond, it was layered at the sides to sweep over and behind his perfectly shaped ears to fall just below his shoulders.

It was a habit of Danni's to liken people to animals and she found herself doing it now with Ivan and Fauve. He reminded her of a pure-bred stallion. Screaming virility from every pore, his body was firm and strong with skin the colour of toast, his carriage erect, his movements supple and fluid, the whole magnificent ensemble crowned by a silky white mane. By the same token, she decided, Fauve was strongly reminiscent of a gazelle. Her figure was delicately proportioned, her movements lithe and graceful and her face, with it's long-lashed, almond-shaped eyes and tiny pink mouth, was so feminine it made Danni almost weep with envy. As for herself, she felt as ungainly as a hippo in comparison.

Thankfully she had no time to ponder her own disadvantages. Fauve led her over to a large group of soft, white cambric-covered sofas where she instructed her to sit. On a low table in front of her Danni could see a collection of old circus programmes and magazines. Leaning forward she picked one up and began to flick idly through it as Fauve and Ivan stood a little way off, talking quietly.

Glancing surreptitiously over the top of the magazine, Danni found her gaze drawn once again to Ivan. He was dressed all in cream, his trousers and casual shirt cut from a fine silky fabric that seemed to flow over his hard, taut body yet disguised nothing. She fancied she could see every ripple, every curve and delineation of his

30

musculature beneath his clothes. All at once she found herself growing very warm and had to fan herself with the magazine to stop herself from feeling faint again.

Unable to bear the physical torment of looking at Ivan any longer, she closed her eyes, revelling instead in the peace and quiet that surrounded her and the scent of fresh flowers which the outstretched arms of a warm breeze carried in from the open windows. Finding herself lulled into blissful contemplation, Danni was surprised when she felt the seat beside her give a little. Opening her eyes she found Fauve was studying her, her expression inscrutable yet bearing the merest hint of a secretive smile. Automatically Danni smiled back at her then glanced up and immediately felt a sharp pang of disappointment – Ivan was nowhere to be seen.

'Oh, he's gone,' she said without meaning to.

Fauve patted her hand indulgently. 'I thought you would take to Ivan. 'E is nice isn't 'e? 'E 'as agreed to be your tutor and mentor during your stay 'ere.'

Danni didn't know whether to laugh or run away. Nice, the woman said, nice? He was gorgeous. And here was Fauve suggesting that she would be spending the next couple of weeks under his metaphorical wing. Quickly, Danni mentally altered Ivan's similarity to that of a golden eagle.

Her smile turned to a grin as she gazed back at the Frenchwoman, noticing for the first time the light floral perfume she wore. 'You'll have to forgive me if I seem a bit nervous,' she said by way of a convincing explanation for her behaviour. 'I haven't ever done anything this daring before.'

'Ah!' Fauve laughed and clapped her hands delightedly. 'You do not know the meaning of daring yet, my dear. Wait until Ivan 'as started putting you through your paces. You will amaze yourself. I guarantee it.'

'I hope so,' Danni said. 'You've been so kind to me already, what with letting me come here at a reduced rate and everything. I promise I'll do my very best and won't let you down.'

Glancing down, Danni watched as Fauve's hand left hers to squeeze her knee reassuringly instead. 'I'm sure. But please don't be too grateful yet, you're 'ere to work as well as 'ave fun, you know.'

'Oh, yes,' Danni agreed, nodding enthusiastically and trying hard not to feel discomfited by the Frenchwoman's overtly tactile gestures, 'I'll do the dishes, cook, make the beds, whatever—'

'You'll do nothing of the sort,' Fauve interrupted her. 'When I say work, I mean at your lessons. 'Ere you will learn skills you never thought possible. And I also 'ope,' she added, in a slightly lower tone, 'that you will discover many new things about yourself at the same time.'

Danni shivered at the way Fauve spoke. Again, her tone and the implication behind her words seemed strangely intimate. All at once, she found herself wondering what it was exactly Fauve and Ivan had in store for her.

'Where will I be sleeping?' she asked to break

the thread of apprehension that threatened to strangle her.

'Oh, my dear, I am so sorry. You must be anxious to – 'ow you say? – wash your hands.' Fauve laughed again and stood up. 'Come with me, Danni.' she said. 'I will show you to your room. Then a little later Ivan will come and get you and show you around properly. The sooner you feel relaxed and at 'ome 'ere the better, no?'

'Yes,' Danni said, thinking she sounded as relieved as she felt, 'thank you. I'm sure everything will be just perfect.'

In the predominantly white bedroom which Fauve had allocated to her – where wide French windows on one side of the room gave her such a feeling of light and space that she felt as though she and the surrounding countryside were one – Danni realised the true meaning of perfection. Everything around her bore the hallmarks of Fauve's style.

At that very moment she was reclining on a huge double bed covered in fine white broderie anglaise which matched the drapes that hung from a brass pole above her head. These were caught either side of the bed by huge bows of oyster ribbon fixed to brass rings, which in turn were cemented into the white plaster wall. The floor was covered by thick, cream carpet. And opposite her was a long pine dressing-table and drawer unit. A white painted door led to a large bathroom complete with a deep claw-footed bath with a shower, a shell-shaped porcelain basin,

33

matching lavatory and a bidet.

So French, she had mused to herself the first time she noticed the bidet. Whereupon she had found herself wondering if she would actually use it for the purpose it was intended, or if she would end up soaking her smalls in it instead, like most English people who were unused to such continental luxuries.

There and then she had resolved to watch Fauve and try to imitate her. It wouldn't do her any harm to learn a little finesse, she decided. If just a tiny amount of the Frenchwoman's chic rubbed off on her it would be to the good. She could just imagine Tam's face if she returned home looking as though she had stepped elegantly from the pages of a French fashion magazine. For a start she would try to do something more interesting with her hair. Although she couldn't imagine herself with a style as short as Fauve's, she could practise pinning it up, or at least braiding it. Long flowing locks, she decided, would definitely be a hindrance to some of the things she planned to learn – like fire-eating for instance. She shuddered as she imagined accidentally setting her golden brown tresses alight at her first attempt.

'Are you cold, Danni – in this heat?'

The voice, all too familiar already, set her pulse racing. Turning her head almost unwillingly, she noticed that Ivan had stepped into her room through one of the pairs of French windows.

'I, er, no, I was just imagining setting my hair alight,' she replied instantly. She felt foolish as she

34

answered him and wondered why she felt compelled to be quite so honest sometimes.

His seductive mouth curved into a smile as he sat down uninvited on the edge of her bed. 'Really, are you that bored?' he said.

Danni gazed back at him. The look he gave her was so lambent she fancied she could feel herself melting from the inside out. Somehow she managed to shake her head.

'No, I—' she began before quickly giving up trying to explain. Instead she said, 'Fauve mentioned something about a guided tour.'

'Ah, yes.' Ivan continued to smile at her, his eyes making an appraising sweep of her reclining body which now stiffened. 'I keep forgetting you are new to all of this. Somehow,' he paused and reached out to stroke a single finger along the sole of her bare foot, 'I feel you are already a part of this – us. You have a certain – oh, I don't know – I suppose Fauve would call it *je ne sais quoi*.'

Danni's eyes widened and she tried not to wriggle her foot. 'Do I?'

'Oh yes.' Ivan's finger moved to her other foot and this time, when he had finished stroking up and down the sole, he began to circle her ankle. 'I see great things for you and me. We will make a good team, I know it.'

As Danni concentrated on the mesmerising effect of his finger, she couldn't help noticing for the first time that he also had a slightly unusual accent.

'Are you French too?' she asked.

'No.' He laughed and to her disappointment took his finger away. 'I am stateless, timeless and therefore ageless.' He stood up and to Danni's surprise stretched his arms wide in a theatrical gesture, as though he were trying to embrace the world. 'This whole earth is my birthplace. I belong wherever I am. And I am whatever I want to be.'

Danni shook her head, wondering if she had actually fallen asleep and was now lost in the depths of a particularly vivid though confusing dream. His laugh brought her back to reality with a jolt.

'Come on,' he said, reaching out a hand to her, 'you must not let me distract you from your reasons for being here.'

'I'm not quite sure what they are, to be truthful,' she admitted, struggling to her feet and casting a searching gaze around the floor for her shoes. She spotted them tucked under a low, armless chair covered in oyster sateen. As she slipped her feet into them she glanced up at him. 'I want to learn as much as I can. I don't know if Fauve told you but I've loved the circus since I was a child.'

'You along with many other people,' Ivan said, leading her through the doorway and around the long, single-storey building. 'The only difference is, you have the courage to explore your dreams.'

Exploring my dreams, Danni mused as she followed him – is that what I'm doing? She realised she felt strangely detached from reality. She hadn't eaten since early that morning yet felt no hunger. Nor was she thirsty. Like Ivan, she simply *was* . . .

36

He took her across the closely mown field behind the farm buildings to the marquee. It looked much bigger close to, Danni realised, than it had from the road. Inside, it was everything she expected from a circus tent, albeit slightly scaled down. From the high canvas ceiling hung a trapeze and two ladders, between which was strung a high wire. Quite a distance below a large orange net was suspended from tall metal poles sunk into the ground. As they drew closer to it, Danni saw that the net was still a good metre or so above her head.

'I will take you up there tomorrow or the next day,' Ivan said, pointing to the top of the ladder where the platform looked about as large as a postage stamp.

'Oh no, I don't think—' Danni started to say but Ivan interrupted her.

'You will trust me, I hope, Danni,' he said. 'No harm will come to you if you place all your faith in me – only pleasure.'

She thrilled to his words and the darkly promising way in which they were said. Trust him? she thought. To trust another human being that much, particularly a man, was asking an awful lot of her.

Fleetingly she recalled a very old memory she had thought was lost to her for ever. It was of her father repeatedly throwing her into the air and catching her again. Then once, just once, he had turned at the last minute, distracted by something her mother called out to him and Danni had fallen to the ground. Fortunately, the grass had not been mown and was long and soft. Nor had she fallen very far. But it had been enough to make her wary.

Years later, when her father had left her and her mother to live with another woman, his betrayal had been enough to revive her mistrust of men and she had vowed from that day forth always to expect the worst and withhold a tiny part of herself from other people. That way they could never hurt her, never let her down.

'You look doubtful,' Ivan said, interrupting her morose thoughts. 'I will cure you of that.'

Oh yes, Danni wanted to retort, suddenly angry with him through no fault of his own – how? But she remained silent in what she hoped was an enigmatic but still interested way. Though she felt angry with men in general, the last thing she wanted to do was put Ivan off her. At least, she reasoned, not until she had given him a fair chance to prove himself.

Chapter Three

DANNI WAS IN the shower when she heard the insistent tapping sound. Turning off the powerful jet of warm water she cocked an ear and listened. There it was again, the sound of knuckles rapping on glass. Quickly she grabbed an oyster pink towel from the rail. Wrapping it around her, she went into the bedroom. Outside the French windows to her right, which she had prudently locked before taking her shower, she could see Ivan with his fist poised to rap on the glass again.

Feeling as embarrassed as a schoolgirl, she hugged the towel closer to her body. Securing it firmly around her bust, she rushed to the window. She fumbled awkwardly with the lock and eventually was forced to stop holding the towel with one arm so that she could turn the handle and open the door.

'Yes?' she said, hovering nervously on the threshold.

She trembled as she stood there, the wet ends of her hair straggling over her shoulders and dripping down her back. As she was barefoot Ivan seemed even taller and more intimidating than before. And though she felt the warmth of his gaze as it cast across her bare throat and shoulders where droplets of water still clung to her lightly browned skin, she couldn't help shivering.

Just as she opened her mouth to repeat her question, he spoke.

'Fauve asked me to tell you that dinner will be served in the main hall at eight,' he said.

Automatically Danni glanced at her bare wrist and realised her watch was lying on the dressing-table, where she had put it before taking her shower.

'It's only a quarter past six,' Ivan supplied for her. 'You've got plenty of time.'

'What do people, er, that is—' Danni cursed herself for stammering. 'What should I wear?'

Again, Ivan treated her to a warm appraisal. This time though his eyes swept the whole of her body in a long, lingering way. Danni felt instantly embarrassed. Although the towel covered her body from bust to knees she still felt incredibly under-dressed.

Apparently ignorant of her discomfort, Ivan leaned casually against the door-frame. 'I would suggest you wear a bit more than that towel,' he said in an amused tone.

This time Danni blushed. She could feel it starting at the tips of her toes and spreading like wild-fire to the roots of her hair.

'I, I wasn't – I'm not—' she stammered again.

She flinched as Ivan reached out and touched her shoulder.

'You are tense, aren't you, little one?' he said.

Danni felt her throat go dry. His voice was as much of a caress as the fingers stroking her bare shoulder. She tried to shrug and regretted it immediately as the top of her towel slipped a little. She felt the flush across her throat increase as Ivan glanced down. Above the edge of the towel the upper swell of her breasts was clearly visible. Gulping, Danni hitched up the front of the towel again and tried hard to look unconcerned.

'I suppose I am a bit wound up,' she admitted when she finally found her voice. 'It's been a long day and this is all so strange.' She glanced around him to suggest that she was referring to their surroundings.

To her embarrassment, Ivan reached up with his other hand and began to stroke both her shoulders. His touch was warm and soothing and Danni could feel herself melting a little as his fingertips started to knead the taut muscles. He was right, she realised, she *was* feeling tense.

'I am an excellent masseur,' he continued immodestly but in a way that made Danni instantly believe him. 'If you like I could prove it. You would feel so much better, I promise you.'

For a moment Danni hesitated, weighing up the situation. Although part of her felt nervous about allowing him to touch her, another part acknowledged that she had always wanted to experience a proper massage and his touch was not unpleasant by any means. There was also the question of having almost two hours to kill before dinner.

'OK,' she agreed. As she nodded she took a step back. Now her body no longer blocked the doorway it was an open invitation to Ivan to enter.

She continued walking backwards and Ivan followed her, stooping as he entered through the French door. Glancing around hurriedly, Danni realised the only place she could lie down comfortably was the bed. The thought sent a shiver of apprehension through her, then she reminded herself that she was an adult and there were other people around. If Ivan did anything she didn't like she only had to yell and someone would probably come running. Not that he would anyway, she told herself firmly as she lay face down on the broderie anglaise bedspread and rested the side of her face on her folded arms, She was far too unsophisticated to interest a man like him.

From her prone position she watched as Ivan closed the door carefully behind him then reached for the tasselled cord hanging beside it. A pair of self-striped oyster silk curtains swished across the glass wall, casting rosy-hued shadows across the cream carpet. She noticed how he glanced around, his noble brow creasing in confusion.

'Is something the matter?' Danni asked from the bed.

He turned his head to look at her and she felt her breath catch as it did every time he fixed her with those piercing blue eyes.

'I was wondering if you had some body lotion,

42

or oil of some kind,' he said.

'There's a bottle of baby oil on the shelf in the bathroom,' Danni offered, 'or I think I've got some—'

He didn't give her chance to finish her sentence. 'Baby oil will be perfect,' he said. Turning away, he walked into the bathroom and returned a moment later with the clear plastic bottle in his hand.

She felt the mattress give as he perched on the side of the bed. Then he uncapped the bottle and poured a little of the oil into the palm of his hand. Putting down the bottle on the bedside table, he began to rub his hands together lightly.

'I'm just warming the oil,' he explained. 'If it's not at body temperature the shock of it can make you feel even more tense.'

Danni nodded gravely. She felt as though her gaze was transfixed by the sight of his long fingers glistening with oil, knowing that in a moment they would come into contact with her bare skin.

In the next moment, as his oily palms swept across her shoulders, the breath she didn't realise she was holding was expelled from her lungs on a long sigh. The pressure of his hands was light but firm, the fingertips moulding themselves around the contours of her muscles, kneading them until they felt as soft and pliable as Plasticine.

'Good?' he asked softly.

Danni felt as though she hardly had the strength to nod. His breath was warm upon her ear. It excited the delicate membranes there, making her shiver inside.

'Very,' she gasped. 'I didn't realise how good a massage could feel.'

'Most people don't until they experience it for the first time,' Ivan said, continuing to knead her shoulders. The pads of his thumbs began to follow the ridges of her spine, smoothing and circling. 'But that can be said of many things,' he added. 'Now, could you lift up your hair – I want to massage your neck.'

Reaching behind her, Danni gathered up her hair obediently and swept it upwards, piling it up on top of her head and holding it there. She kept the side of her face pressed against the pillow. As Ivan's thumbs travelled further up her spine to the very base of her hairline, she felt her eyelids growing heavy. In fact, she mused dreamily, her whole body felt heavy. Leaden with drowsiness, it seemed to be sinking deeper and deeper into the mattress.

His touch was magical, driving away all traces of the strain and pressure which had taken their toll over the past few months: work, lack of money, her problems with Tam . . . All at once, Danni felt a flare of warmth in her lower belly. Ivan's fingertips were still massaging her neck, gently easing the taut muscles at the base where it met her shoulders, but now it seemed as though small threads made a direct connection from her neck to her lower body. The nape of her neck was an erogenous zone, she knew that full well, but she hadn't realised how sensitive it was until this moment.

The desire she felt was unmistakable. Its

warmth flooded her, melting her from the inside out. She could feel gentle trickles of moisture seeping out of her as it gathered in her newly awakened vagina. Pressed against the soft towelling, her clitoris began to swell and pulse. Oh, God, no – not now, she prayed silently, wondering how her body could betray her so readily when only a short while before her mind had been concerned about Ivan taking advantage of her. He had continued to behave like a perfect gentleman, confining the promised massage to her neck and shoulders. Whereas she seemed to be behaving like a depraved beast. Despite her best intentions her body worked of its own accord – blossoming, moistening, becoming warmer and warmer and no doubt giving off the unmistakable scent of arousal.

'I think that will do,' she gasped hastily, struggling to sit up.

Ivan's palm flat against her upper back pinned her down. 'Nonsense,' he said. 'I haven't done your arms yet.'

'My arms are fine,' Danni insisted, still struggling. 'Please!' She felt the release of pressure as Ivan took his hand away and sat back. When she rolled over onto her side, she noticed that he was looking at her with a curious expression.

'What's the matter?' he asked simply.

'The time,' Danni said lamely. 'It must be getting late.'

She felt completely flustered as she watched him glance at his wristwatch again.

'It's only five to seven,' he said. Although he

looked perplexed he made no further comment. Instead he stood up and returned the bottle of baby oil to the bathroom. Then he hovered by the French windows, where the curtains were still drawn. 'I'll see you later, at dinner,' he murmured to her as he reached into the gap between the curtains for the handle.

Still lying on the bed Danni watched him push open the door. For some reason she felt guilty, but couldn't understand why.

'Yes, OK,' she said, clearing her throat, which felt extraordinarily tight. Then, almost as an afterthought – by which time he was halfway through the door, she called out, 'And thank you – for the massage, I mean.'

His white-blond head swivelled around and she noticed, with relief, that he was smiling as he looked at her over his shoulder.

'Don't mention it,' he said lightly. 'Any time.'

It was only when dinner-time finally arrived that Danni realised she had no idea where the 'great hall' was. She knocked tentatively on the front door of the main farmhouse and when there was no reply walked around to the back where she found that the stable-type kitchen door was standing wide open. As she popped her head around she saw two identical young women standing side by side chopping tomatoes and red peppers. The colour of the vegetables, she noticed, almost matched the shade of their straight, shoulder-length hair.

They glanced up and the one nearest to the door smiled at her and said, 'You must be new. Are you lost?'

Danni nodded. 'I'm looking for the great hall.'

The young woman put down her chopping knife and picked up a blue and white checked towel. Rubbing her hands on it she inclined her head towards a heavy wooden door on the far side of the huge kitchen.

'Straight through there,' she said amiably. 'I think Fauve and a couple of the others are already waiting.'

Murmuring her thanks Danni walked across the wide expanse of red flagstone covered floor, noticing on her way that the kitchen was typically rustic. Heavy oak beams supported the low ceiling and were festooned with strings of garlic and dried herbs. Along the wall to her right oak cuboards sat either side of a huge black kitchen range. And in the centre of the room stood a long, scrubbed oak table surrounded by matching wheelbacked chairs.

The twin girls were standing in front of another range of cupboards which were topped by a white marble work surface and a double sink. In one of the basins a stainless steel colander was heaped with lettuce leaves, on which water droplets still clung, glistening like fat diamonds. The other basin contained an assortment of dirty cooking utensils. The two young women looked very youthful indeed in their pink overalls, which somehow failed to clash with their hair, and very slim.

47

'Do you need any help?' Danni felt compelled to ask. It seemed to her that, depite Fauve's protestations, she should be doing more to pay for her keep than enjoying warm showers and long massages.

The two shook their red heads simultaneously. 'Oh, no, you're here to learn, not work,' they chorused.

Danni couldn't help noticing how they glanced at each other straight afterwards and seemed to share a knowing look. It made her feel distinctly uncomfortable without knowing why. Take no notice, it's just your overactive imagination at work again, she told herself firmly. Nevertheless, as she pushed open the door and stepped through it, she was sure it wasn't her imagination when she heard one of them say to the other, 'Like a lamb to the slaughter.' Nor did she imagine the light tinkle of girlish laughter that followed.

As she stepped into the room beyond, closing the door hastily behind her to block out the echoes of laughter that seemed to follow in her wake, she realised the term 'great hall' was an anomaly. Hardly larger than the bedroom she had been allocated, this room was perhaps the most sparsely furnished she had seen so far – with only a round polished table encircled by eight straight-backed chairs. The walls were natural brick, relieved only by a few strategically hung paintings, and the flooring was bare wooden boards. Only the fire burning merrily in a cast-iron grate gave the room any feeling of warmth and habitation.

Another door on the far side opened at that

moment and in walked Fauve, dressed in smart black trousers and a matching silky blouse. A smile lit up her face as she noticed Danni hovering uncertainly and she extended a fine-boned hand in greeting.

'Danni, 'ow lovely you look, come and sit,' Fauve said.

Danni glanced down at herself. Compared with the chic Frenchwoman she didn't feel all that lovely. Unsure what she should wear, she had opted for one of her two dresses. T-shirt style, it was made of white ribbed cotton and had shoe-string straps and a scooped neckline. As she had forgotton to pack any tights she was bare-legged. Her only concession to dressing up had been to put on a pair of gold high-heeled sandals.

'I didn't know what I should wear,' she managed to blurt out, 'especially as I hadn't thought to bring any smart clothes.' Crossing the room, she sat on one of the dining chairs and clasped her hands demurely in her lap.

Fauve took the chair next to hers. Pausing to smooth imaginary creases from her trousers, she crossed her legs elegantly and turned her body slightly so that she was facing Danni.

'What you 'ave chosen is *parfait*,' she said, reaching out to finger one of Danni's shoestring straps. 'That colour, it look so good with your tan and it 'ug your figure like a lover.' Danni blushed at the comparison and forced herself to remain calm as one of Fauve's pink-tipped fingernails scraped lightly across her throat. 'It just lack the jewels,'

Fauve added, 'do you not 'ave any – a gold chain perhaps and some earrings?' She flicked Danni's tawny hair over her shoulder as she spoke, exposing a bare earlobe which she regarded with a narrow-eyed look of dissatisfaction.

Danni used the shake of her head to dislodge the Frenchwoman's hand. 'I'm not really a jewellery person,' she said, 'but I normally do wear earrings. I just forgot to put them in after my shower, that's all.' She watched as Fauve sat back and appraised her thoughtfully.

'Are you pierced anywhere else?' Fauve asked out of the blue.

Taken aback by the question, Danni found herself blushing and stammering as she answered, 'No, I haven't – I couldn't—'

Fauve laughed huskily. 'It can be very becoming,' she assured Danni, 'the nipples, the labia, even the delicate little clitoris can all look very pretty when adorned.' She paused and raised her head, glancing toward the doorway as Ivan entered. '*N'est-ce pas*, Ivan?' she said, drawing him into the conversation as he took the empty chair next to Danni.

'What is that, *ma chérie*?' he asked.

Smiling at him, Fauve repeated what she had just told Danni.

'Oh, yes,' he said, nodding his affirmation to Danni, who blushed even deeper. She wished fervently that they weren't having this conversation 'Such beautiful parts look even more beautiful decorated with gold and precious gems,' he continued.

'I don't really think that's for me,' Danni said, clearing her throat hastily. She glanced around, wishing she had something to drink. Her throat felt awfully dry. It was the fault of her damned imagination again. Conjuring visions of all the naked women Ivan must have seen, all of them wearing gold hoops through their pretty pink nipples and their labia studded with diamonds. She forced her mind to dispel the image. 'But then each to his or her own,' she managed to add lightly. She allowed her brave words to die away, realising that Ivan and Fauve were both gazing at her intently.

Thankfully, at that moment, the door opened again and a thin young man appeared. Like Fauve he was dressed all in black and his collar-length hair was as sleek and dark as his clothing. As she watched him sit next to Fauve, Danni realised that the red-headed twins were the only two people she had seen so far at the circus school who looked and sounded English. She could tell by this young man's olive complexion and his chocolatey irises that he was foreign.

Fauve smiled at the young man then turned to Danni. 'You haven't met Guido yet, have you, *ma chérie*?' she said. 'He is Italian and absolutely superb on the high wire.'

Danni thought Fauve made it sound as though being Italian and a trapeze artist was a natural combination.

'Really?' she said, reaching across Fauve to offer Guido her hand. 'Nice to meet you, Guido.'

To her delight, the young Italian didn't shake her hand but raised it to his lips. As he cast his eyes down, Danni noticed how thick and silky his lashes were. Inside she felt an envious yearning that almost overrode the flicker of desire she felt as his sulky lips caressed the back of her hand.

Suddenly, it seemed the room was filling with people. The red-headed twins were the next to arrive. They had dispensed with their overalls and were now dressed identically in loose tie-die cotton dresses that reached their ankles. Then two other men entered. Both of them wore dark blue casual trousers and light coloured shirts and both were in their late twenties, Danni estimated. One looked distinctly Scandinavian, if his colouring was anything to go by, and the other had long chestnut hair, caught at the nape of his neck in a ponytail. They also had a similar physique: fairly tall and athletic with muscular arms and shoulders, and flat stomachs that tapered to narrow hips.

Danni couldn't fail to let her interest show. As far as she could remember, there had never been a time when she had been surrounded by such exclusively beautiful people. Usually at social gatherings her lot was the fat, balding accountant, or the hairy macho type. Even the women she normally encountered were flawed in comparison to the female company present tonight. If only I could be like them, she mused ruefully to herself as Guido reached across the table to pour her a glass of wine. She nodded her thanks and was gratified to receive a wolfish smile in return. Whatever her own failings, she told herself as she raised the glass to her lips, things were definitely looking up.

Her attention was diverted by Ivan as he leaned across the space behind her chair to speak to Fauve. One of his hands rested lightly on her shoulder and she couldn't fail to pick up the enticing scent of his citrus and musk aftershave. Trying to ignore the fingers that seemed to be branding her bare skin, Danni concentrated on sipping her wine – a rich, fruity red of some kind – and pretended to study a painting of a circus horse which hung on the far wall. Despite the babble of lively chatter that circulated the table, she couldn't fail to hear what Ivan and Fauve were saying to each other.

'Who is serving dinner tonight?' Ivan asked in an undertone.

'Meah,' Fauve replied. 'She arrive from Mauritius last night. All day she sleep, now she is awake and ready for some fun.'

Danni heard Ivan's low burst of laughter. It sounded indecent somehow, as though Fauve had made a suggestive remark.

'That's good,' Ivan said, 'it seems like a long time since we last had the pleasure of Meah. What a wonderful pupil she turned out to be.'

'Ah, *absolument*,' Fauve agreed, '*mais notre petite amie*, she will appreciate such fun?'

Her words ended on a questioning note and although Danni's French wasn't all that good, she recognised enough to know Fauve had some misgivings that concerned her. A sense of intrigue mingled with that of trepidation, caused Danni's stomach to churn. Fortunately, she didn't have long to ponder her fate. At that moment the door opened again and this time a young woman she hadn't seen before entered, pushing a trolley laden with food.

Dressed in a traditional French maid's costume, with a skirt that was barely decent, the young woman had a wonderfully exotic appearance. Skin the colour of tobacco shimmered like silk over slender limbs. Her face was a beguiling heart shape in which almond eyes were set like jewels either side of a small, neat nose. Her mouth, painted a deep plum colour, was generous and bore a slight pout that Danni would come to recognise as natural. But her hair was her crowning glory in every sense: long and dark, it flowed over her shoulders and down her back like a satin sheet, the wispy ends just reaching the base of her spine.

As she reached the table with the trolley, she stood up, showing how the mass of frothy white petticoats under the black silk of her skirt barely reached the tops of her thighs.

Glancing first at Fauve and then at Ivan, she licked her plummy lips provocatively. 'Dinner is served,' she said in a thickly accented voice. She waved a slender hand over the feast. 'Please, *mesdames et messieurs*, enjoy.'

All at once the dull little room was filled with the lively chatter of cutlery on porcelain. While

Guido and Ivan began to lift the heavy dishes from the trolley and place them on the table, the maid stalked over to the fireplace on impossibly high black heels. There she picked up a silver candelabrum and brought it back to the table, where she lit the five red candles.

Moving to the far wall, she flicked off the electric light and all at once the room was cloaked in intimacy. The light from the candles and the flickering fire now cast a rosy glow over the plain white tablecloth, glinting off the heavy silver cutlery and turning the cut-crystal glasses to rainbow-hued prisms.

Already feeling light-headed from the potency of the wine on an empty stomach, Danni almost reeled from the effect. Even though it was a good seven or eight feet away and was blocked by the bodies of the twins, the fire seemed to be giving out a lot of warmth. Without realising what she was doing, Danni pulled at the front of her dress where it seemed to be sticking to her breasts.

'Interesting,' Ivan said in her ear. 'No bra.'

Yet again, Danni felt herself blushing furiously. 'I can't wear one with this dress,' she said in a deliberately casual tone. 'It's the straps.'

'Then we should all thank the good Lord for your straps,' Ivan said to her, raising his glass as if in a toast.

Disconcerted by his interest and by the way her body was betraying her – her sex moistening and sending out urgent signals – Danni lowered her eyes to her plate and pretended to become absorbed with the food in front of her. At any other time she would have been delighted by the food: a harmonious concoction of thinly sliced chicken breasts in a cream and mushroom sauce, generously laced with white wine, heaped over ribbons of garlic and herb tagliatelle. As it was, she could hardly remember tasting a thing. Ignoring the crisp green salad that was served the French way, as a second course, she reached greedily for one of the bottles of wine that seemed to be circulating freely.

'I'd go easy on that, if I were you, it's potent stuff,' an unfamiliar voice said in her ear.

Turning her head, Danni noticed that the Scandinavian was hovering by her shoulder. Ivan was talking with one of the twins, who had moved to sit next to him while they were waiting for dessert to be served, so Danni flashed the newcomer an encouraging smile.

'Dutch courage,' she said, waving the bottle. 'Are you Dutch?' She noticed, when he grinned broadly, that he had very white teeth. Instantly, the sight of them reminded her of Tam and she found herself backing off a little mentally. With his floppy blond hair, he reminded her quite a lot of Tam, she realised.

'No, Norwegian,' he said. 'My name's Randi, what's yours?'

Despite her intention to stay cool, Danni laughed. 'Danielle,' she said, 'although everyone calls me Danni.'

His eyes were the colour of denim, she noticed

56

as they creased up at the corners. 'Why did you laugh, Danni?' he asked.

For a moment she couldn't remember and she gazed blankly at him. 'Oh,' she said as the memory came back, 'it was your name.'

He cocked his head to one side, looking endearingly puppyish. 'Randi is a funny name?'

'It is for someone English,' the twin who had been talking to Ivan cut in from across the table. 'Mind you,' she added, giving him a frank look of appraisal, 'it suits you.'

Feeling as though she were caught up in a game of verbal tennis, Danni glanced from one to the other.

'I'm Lettie, short for Letitia,' the twin continued, shifting her gaze to Danni, and that's my sister Rose sitting over there talking to Aldous. Our parents were only prepared name-wise for one red-haired baby and Rose came out first, so she got the name they had chosen.'

Danni smiled at Lettie, thinking how nice and normal she seemed compared with Fauve and Ivan, even Guido and Randi. 'Do you come from around here?' she asked.

'Just up the road,' Lettie said. 'When we saw that the circus school had started up in the village me and Rose ran away from home.'

Marvelling at the sisters' daring, Danni said, 'How old were you when you ran away?'

Lettie sat back and gazed blankly up at the ceiling, giving the impression that she was counting in her head. 'We'll be twenty this August,' she said finally, reverting her gaze to Danni, 'and this'll be our second summer, so we must have been seventeen, nearly eighteen.'

All at once Danni felt quite old. She could just about remember turning twenty.

'And you, my dear Danni, how old are you?' Ivan interrupted as though he could read her thoughts.

As if a light had just been switched on inside her, Danni felt herself warming instantly again. 'Twenty-six. An old woman,' she joked. To her delight, Ivan took her hand and cradled it in his own.

'Not old, Danni,' he admonished her gently, 'but certainly old enough.'

Thrilling to the dark promise that lurked in his tone, Danni found herself once again drawn to his gaze. It was true, she told herself, she was old enough. Certainly of an age where she could stop acting like a gauche teenager and start appreciating the attentions of a charming, not to mention extremely gorgeous man.

Chapter Four

DESSERT WAS A fresh fruit salad, served in cut-glass bowls, with a generous dollop of whipped cream on top. Danni eyed the temptation put in front of her by the exotic Meah and in an unconscious gesture patted her stomach.

'Worrying about your figure?' Ivan whispered in her ear.

Glancing sideways at him, Danni gave him an abashed smile. 'I've been watching my weight lately,' she admitted, 'my boyfriend—'

'Must be an idiot if he doesn't appreciate you just the way you are,' Ivan finished for her, adding, 'You're gorgeous, every inch of you.' His smile was slow and warm as he picked up her spoon, scooped up half a strawberry and a little of the cream and held it to her lips.

Danni hesitated. She wasn't used to such blatant flattery, nor to being spoonfed by a virtual stranger. Still, she opened her mouth obediently and experienced a delicious thrill of pleasure as the succulent fruit slipped onto her tongue. As she chewed and swallowed she kept her gaze locked with Ivan's. For just that moment it seemed as though they were the only two people in the room. Everything, everyone else receded into insignificance as she felt herself drowning in his deep blue eyes. Seemingly of its own accord her body inclined towards his. She realised she would have to relax and learn to trust him, as he had suggested. Otherwise the next two weeks would be a waste of everybody's time, not to mention Fauve's generosity.

'You're too kind,' she murmured, accepting another mouthful of fruit from the proffered spoon. Her teeth clashed on the silver spoon, sending a frisson through her.

Putting down the spoon, Ivan picked up a napkin instead and dabbed at the corners of her mouth.

'Not kind,' he said, 'merely honest.' He laid the napkin back down but continued to gaze intently at her. 'I don't ever say things I don't mean.'

As Danni nodded, she acknowledged how desperately she wanted to believe him. For most of her life she had felt at a disadvantage because of her figure. In the early days of puberty her child's body had seemed to suddenly transform itself into that of a woman in one gigantic leap. Not for her a slow series of changes: the budding protuberances of breasts, the delicate fuzz of hair that gradually thickened. Overnight, it seemed, she had become a fully fledged woman.

Along with the change wrought on her had

come a host of confused emotions. Grown men started taking an interest in her, making her feel at a terrible disadvantage because her body responded in ways that her mind could not cope with. Later, when she finally ceded her virginity at the ripe old age of sixteen and a half she had immediately embarked on a sexual spree, bedding nearly every man or boy who showed an interest in her. Then had come a couple of years' remorse and near celibacy, followed by her relationship with Tam.

Now, she realised, she had never really allowed herself the luxury of proper sexual adventure and by that she meant slow seduction and true sensuality. After her early forays, she had settled for the sort of half pleasure Tam had offered. All at once she saw that her feelings for Tam had been based on gratitude. Gratitude for saving her from the twin evils of promiscuity and celibacy. Her feminine instincts told her that another kind of erotic enjoyment existed. She just hadn't discovered it yet. Somehow she recognised that perhaps Fauve and Ivan and their oddly assorted troupe held the key.

She gave Ivan a lopsided smile as he softly spoke to her again.

'I'm sorry, I didn't catch that,' she said.

His fingers stroked the length of her bare arm, the tips of them stopping at her wrist to describe small circles on the sensitive flesh there.

'I asked you where you had gone,' he said gently. 'You looked as though you were away with the fairies.'

Danni chuckled. 'I was indulging myself in a bit of introspection,' she said. Several glasses of the heady wine meant her tongue had difficulty forming the word.

'And what was your conclusion?' Ivan asked.

He looked intently at her, she noticed, as though he was genuinely interested in the workings of her psyche.

Her natural diffidence made her hesitate. 'I just came to the conclusion that I haven't really learned how to live,' she confided after a moment. 'But that stops as from now.'

She watched as his eyes darkened slightly, the pupils expanding, the colour of the irises deepening to navy. That and the wolfish curve of his lips made her feel warm and desirous. Beneath her dress she felt her breasts swelling. Glancing down, she wasn't surprised to note that her nipples were jutting unashamedly through the thin white cotton.

It was with a certain amount of relief that she saw Fauve lean across to interrupt them.

'We are talking on the subject of *la sensualité*,' she said in the husky voice that Danni envied. 'Guido claims the Italians are masters of the art.'

Beside Danni, Ivan gave a throaty chuckle. 'You would say that, wouldn't you?' He directed his words at the young Italian, who gave a knowing smirk. 'Personally, I think people of all nationalities are capable of great sensuality – even the English.'

Danni noticed how he winked broadly at the

twins. as though he knew what sort of reaction his statement would provoke.

'Pig!' Lettie retorted, 'You foreigners don't have the monopoly on sensuality. Rose and I have learned how to appreciate the finer things in life – as well you know.' The two girls shared a knowing smile which they then flashed around the table.

Only Danni felt excluded.

'Then give me six examples of a truly sensual experience,' Ivan challenged. Resting his forearms on the table, he clasped his hands together and gave the twins a defiant look as he added, 'Non-sexual.'

A whisper of admiration ran around the table but the twins apparently refused to let Ivan's challenge faze them.

'Well, let's see.' As Rose and Lettie spoke they reclined in their chairs in perfect harmony. Then they turned their faces up to study the ceiling, as though the inspiration they sought was written across it.

'Wet leaves,' Rose said, looking forward again. Her green eyes sparkled. 'Remember what it's like to walk in the woods on a crisp autumn morning? The smell of damp leaves and bracken is delicious.'

'And the scent of the earth beneath them,' Lettie added enthusiastically, 'so peaty. Oh, and the texture of it – do you remember that time we stripped off and rubbed it into our bodies, Rose?'

Danni shifted uncomfortably on her chair as she watched the young women go into raptures over the shared reminiscence. It seemed their experience went far beyond the simple strolls through the woods she had enjoyed. All at once she envied them their imaginations and their spirit. Since when would she have thought of rubbing damp earth into her naked body? Glancing hastily sideways she noticed Ivan appeared rapt.

'Go on,' he said. 'That's one.'

'Two,' the twins chorused.

'OK,' Ivan conceded, 'two then. But I still want to hear four more examples.'

Lettie giggled. 'Only four – we've got heaps.'

'The sun,' Rose chipped in suddenly. 'Glowing heat caressing your naked body.'

'Or snow,' Lettie interrupted. 'Rolling around in it in the buff last winter was wonderful.'

Rose nodded, her expression showing how much pleasure that particular recollection gave her. Then she added, 'Chocolate fondue's another one. Letting it cool a little then dripping it slowly onto breasts and thighs—'

'Then licking it off. Mmm . . .' Lettie made a noise of appreciation and licked her lips lasciviously.

Danni glanced around wildly, wondering if everyone was starting to feel as hot and uncomfortable as her. Good God, she asked herself, does everything they do involve them being naked?

'One last one,' Ivan said, appearing unperturbed by the mantle of eroticism that seemed to have descended over the small gathering.

The twins pretended to think hard, although

Danni could tell they were not short of ideas.

'Sawdust,' they said in unison, reminding everyone that they were at a circus school. 'Falling into a huge pile of it from a great height,' Lettie added.

'Don't tell me,' Danni interrupted in an ironic tone. 'You have to be naked to appreciate it.'

The silence that followed was deafening. Then Ivan turned his head slowly to look at her. 'The expression that seems most apt at this moment,' he said smoothly, 'is don't knock it until you've tried it.'

There was no censure in his voice but Danni felt as ashamed and embarrassed as if he had lashed out at her physically. Speaking without thinking was another of the things she loathed about herself.

'Excuse me,' she said hoarsely, pushing back her chair, 'I think I've probably had too much to drink. I should go to bed.'

She missed the raised eyebrows as she stumbled to her feet and made for the door. Grappling with the knob she turned it and headed left down the passageway. It was several minutes later when she realised she didn't know where the hell she was going. I'm lost, she wailed silently, leaning against the wall. Huge tears of frustration ran down her cheeks and she dashed them away angrily with the back of her hand.

'What's all this, Danni?' a familiar voice said. It came to her out of the shadows. 'There was no need to run away. We are all friends. We can take a joke without any hard feelings.'

'It just slipped out,' Danni mumbled. 'I didn't mean to be rude.'

She was relieved when Ivan stepped out of the darkness and put out a hand to stroke her hair. 'Of course you didn't,' he said. 'We understood that. It is clear you do not have a malicious bone in your body.'

A harsh laugh tore from her throat but she still managed a wobbly smile. 'I wouldn't say that exactly,' she said. 'I can be a terrible bitch.'

She glanced down at the pale carpeting beneath her feet. 'But I didn't mean to be bitchy then.'

Ivan's hand continued to stroke her hair. 'I know,' he said soothingly, 'don't worry.' His hand left her hair to trace the soft line of her jaw. Three slender fingertips tilted up her chin. 'Do you want to come back with me, or shall I escort you to your room?'

She shook her head regretfully. 'I can't face them again tonight,' she admitted in a small voice. 'I feel like an idiot. Hopefully they'll have forgotten all about it by the morning.'

Gazing deep into her eyes, he smiled. 'You can be sure of that,' he said. 'They are nice people. They don't take offence. Now,' he paused to take her arm and glance around, 'we need to go this way.'

Feeling embarrassed, Danni tried to shake his hand off. 'You don't need to take me,' she insisted, 'just point me in the right direction. Then you can go back to enjoying yourself.'

He regarded her with a quizzical expression, then said something that made her stomach turn to water. 'If you think I don't enjoy being with you, Danni, you are very much mistaken. You are the loveliest young woman I have met in a long time – outside and in,' he added emphatically. 'You are too hard on yourself and I think you have been hurt, no?'

At that moment, Danni thought, he sounded more French than Fauve. 'Yes,' she said, nodding, 'but I'll get over it. I'm almost there already.'

They began to walk down the long passageway, turning right and left at intervals. As they walked, Danni found herself confiding in Ivan about her earlier reminiscences, particularly her confusion at being transformed from a child to a woman in one fell swoop and the pain she had felt. It seemed completely natural to be talking to him in that way. She supposed it was because he was so easy to be with. To her, he wasn't a man she hardly knew but a compassionate person who offered her friendship. Although perhaps, she dared to admit to herself as they left the farmhouse and walked across the courtyard, she wouldn't mind if he offered her something more.

When they reached her room Ivan seemed in no hurry to get back to Fauve and the others. He took the key from her trembling hand and unlocked the door. Stepping into the room ahead of her, he walked to the bedside table and flicked on the lamp. The red bulb, which Danni hadn't noticed before, immediately cast a rosy glow upon the white walls and ceiling. Then he walked around the bed and switched on the other lamp.

Now the room that was bright and airy by day seemed cosy and womb-like. As Danni glanced around she couldn't help noticing how soft and inviting the bed looked. Like the rest of the room, the broderie anglaise covering was cast with a blush pink hue that beguiled her. Heedless of Ivan's presence, Danni kicked off her shoes and sat on the bed. After a moment, while he stood in the centre of the room, she reclined back on her elbows and regarded him thoughtfully. His gaze as he stared back at her was so lambent she felt her body melting. She remained unaware that her desire glowed around her, reaching out to him with ethereal arms.

'You are so beautiful, Danni,' Ivan said in a voice filled with wonder. 'If only you could see yourself as others see you.'

'Now that's a gift everyone would like to have,' she replied in a tone so light she marvelled at her capacity for sounding cool when inside she felt volcanic. Emotion churned inside her in a way that it never had before. She wanted Ivan, she realised. She wanted him to stay and talk to her some more. She wanted him to hold her, caress her, make love to her. Suddenly she shivered, thinking he must be able to see the desire in her eyes and the way her body sent out voluptuous signals.

Glancing down she noticed how far up her thighs her dress had ridden. Another inch and she would be displaying the semi-transparent whiteness of her knickers. When she looked up she noticed she had unintentionally drawn Ivan's attention to her bare legs. She kicked her feet idly, enjoying his attention.

For once, she realised, she felt completely calm and in control. It was as though she had known all along that they would reach this point sooner or later. And she thanked her lucky stars that it seemed to be sooner. The monotony of working in a stuffy office and travelling on the Tube every day seemed such a stark contrast to the sophisticated yet relaxed atmosphere around her now. It was as if the very act of enrolling in the circus school had helped her cross an invisible chasm between the mundane and the new and exciting.

'Would you like a drink?' she asked, wondering why he was still standing a few feet away from her when it was obvious that she wanted him to be much closer. Daringly, she patted the space beside her on the bed. 'If you want to sit down I'll get us something.'

'Just a soft drink,' Ivan said, moving to the bed.

As he sat down Danni got up. She felt the warmth of his gaze on her back as she opened one of the cupboards under the long dressing-table and took out a couple of glasses and one of the bottles of mineral water she had brought with her.

'That's just as well because this is all I've got,' she said with a broad smile as she held up the bottle.

He returned her smile full measure as he nodded. 'Perfect,' he said, 'just like you.'

Danni felt her cheeks dimpling with pleasure and her hand shook slightly as she poured the water. Walking back to the bed, she sat down tentatively and handed Ivan his glass.

'Cheers,' he said softly, touching his glass to hers.

They sipped in silence for a while, allowing themselves to become immersed in the mood of the late evening. The air temperature was still balmy and through the slightly open French window came the rich loamy scent of the surrounding fields and the faint bleating of sheep.

'This is idyllic,' she said, allowing her head to drop back. 'It's so peaceful here, not like London.'

'I can't imagine living in the city,' Ivan said as he put down his glass. 'There is so much pressure and the noise—' He made a disparaging sound and shook his head as if to dispel the unpleasant image.

Danni smiled. Copying Ivan, she put down her glass. Then she turned to him, the expression on her face an open invitation.

'I think I'm going to really enjoy the next couple of weeks,' she said frankly, 'and I don't just mean because of the surroundings. The people too are—' She was forced to break off suddenly as Ivan reached for her and pulled her into his arms.

That first touch of his lips as they met hers was so piquant Danni heard herself groan with longing. Wrapping her arms around his neck she pulled him to her fiercely, her passion surging. She kissed him back forcefully, her tongue darting into his mouth, thrusting and parrying with his as their lips ground together. Locked tightly together, she could feel her breasts pressing against the hard wall of his chest. All at once the thin layers of fabric between them seemed like an unwelcome barrier between pleasure and pure bliss.

Now Danni felt a real empathy with Lettie and Rose's delight at being naked. Only the sensation of her bare skin touching Ivan's, she thought, could improve on the wonder of his kiss. Scrabbling hungrily with her fingertips, she managed to pull his shirt free of his waistband and she sighed softly as her hands encountered his bare flesh. Smooth and hairless, it felt like silk under her fingertips. As she slid her palms up his back as far as she could reach, she delighted in the sensation of his hard musculature and the ridges of his spine. Her hands roamed his back feverishly while his mouth continued to press hot and wet against hers. In the next moment his fingers began raking through her hair and caressing the sensitive area of bare skin between her shoulder-blades.

Heat flared inside her, the plaintive bleating from outside now echoing her own whimpers of arousal. Please, oh yes, her mind urged. Never had the need for physical contact been so strong, she thought. She fancied she could feel him restraining himself, as though he feared he might frighten her if he were to let loose the full force of his passion.

'Don't hold back,' she murmured, pulling her mouth away from his. 'I want you, all of you.'

With a groan he pushed her away from him,

throwing her back against the bed. Taken by surprise, she fell, gasping for breath, her legs sprawling. Excitement churned inside her as she felt his hands roaming her body over the top of her skimpy dress. Her chest heaved and she felt her breasts swelling as his hands covered them.

'My God, Danni, you're gorgeous,' he said huskily, 'so ripe, so delectable.' As he spoke his fingers moulded the pliant flesh of her breasts, his palms rubbing her nipples into ardent little bullets that seemed to be forcing their way through the thin cotton.

'Suck them,' Danni cried out, her own hands pulling down the neckline of her dress. Hungrily she thrust her bared breasts into his face. 'Please, suck them.'

Darts of pure eroticism flashed through her entire body as she saw the darkly passionate look in his eyes and felt the luscious warmth of his lips as they enclosed one nipple. He sucked greedily, drawing the sensitive little nub of flesh into his mouth and lathing it with his tongue. Danni writhed against him, drawing her fingers through his long hair as he mouthed each nipple in turn.

Her dress had ridden right up over her hips by this time and as Ivan finally pulled away she noticed how his expression darkened even further as his glance swept over her body. Following his gaze she saw how flushed and swollen her breasts looked, the nipples so hard and distended it seemed they might burst at any moment. Below the wide ribbed cotton belt that had been her dress, she could see her white knickers stretched tightly across her hips. The dark blonde thatch of her pubic hair showed clearly through the gauzy fabric that clung damply to her crotch.

'My God, Danni,' Ivan said again and she marvelled at the way a man as eloquent as he could suddenly become lost for words. It thrilled her to realise that she was the reason for his loss of speech. The knowledge making her feel even more aroused.

Squirming voluptuously on the bedspread, she spread her thighs a little wider, tilting her pelvis to make him an offering of her body. Look at me, she demanded silently, take this gift and enjoy the pleasure. Although she behaved with a wantonness she had almost forgotten existed, Danni felt strangely submissive in Ivan's presence. Willing and wanting she might be, but she craved the luxury of being erotically dominated. She wanted him to take her and bend her to his will. From that point on she realised that, for as long as he desired, she would be his willing pupil and a slave to his passion.

'Do you want me?' she asked thickly, thinking, please say yes, I want you to want me.

To her relief Ivan nodded, his expression wolfish as he looked deeply into her eyes. The understanding that was transmitted silently between them was unmistakable, a pact that was sealed and remained only to be delivered.

She felt herself trembling as he glanced down and ran his palm possessively over her lower belly.

Slipping his hand between her thighs he rubbed the damp cotton against her crotch.

'Naughty,' he said, darkly. 'So innocent and yet so wet.'

Danni whimpered, feeling herself melt under the heat of her desire for him. Digging her heels into the bed she raised her hips, rubbing herself urgently against his hand. She moaned when he slipped a finger between her outer labia, pressing the thin fabric into the groove between them and caressing the sensitive flesh. A rush of warmth flooded her pelvis as she felt his fingertip stimulating her clitoris. Then shame gripped her as she felt a surge of her own juices soak into the crotch of her knickers, knowing that he would quickly discover the way her body betrayed her.

As his finger slipped lower, urging the sodden fabric into the grasping entrance of her vagina she writhed against him, moaning incoherently. The curve of his lips and the flash in his deep blue eyes were as thrilling as they were wicked.

'You are a tempting little morsel, aren't you?' he said, his fingers working inside her. 'You don't know how difficult it's been for me to resist you. I wanted you the first moment I laid eyes on you.'

Hearing the proof of his desire for her, knowing now that she hadn't imagined the charge of eroticism that had flared between them the moment they met, sent a further rush of pleasure careering through her. She answered him with a groan and churned her pelvis more anxiously, grinding herself down on his probing fingers. The crotch of her knickers was sodden now, the material slippery with her own juices as he rubbed it against her inner walls.

At that moment he hooked his fingers and, probing still further, found the sensitive place high up behind her pubic bone. As he caressed it with knowing dexterity she felt herself soaring on a great wave of pleasure. A pleasure so poignant it was almost painful in its intensity.

'Aah!' she cried, writhing against him. Almost demented with arousal she clutched at her own breasts, massaging the naked orbs urgently between her hands. Plucking at her burning nipples she felt them harden and lengthen even more.

'There is just too much of you to cope with, isn't there, sweetheart?' Ivan said softly. Withdrawing his fingers, he began to tug at the waistband of her knickers. 'Come on, my love, lift your *derrière* – I want to take these off.'

Danni raised her hips obligingly then, and after he had pulled the damp scrap of material down her legs, kicked her panties off. She didn't bother to look and see where they landed but threw herself against him, her fingers fumbling with the clasp on his belt. After a few frustrating moments she managed to work it free and unfasten his trousers. With shameful eagerness she plunged her hands into his pants and was delighted to find that he was already hugely erect.

'What a compliment,' she murmured as she smiled at him.

Her glance took in the mirror over the dressing-table on the far wall and she couldn't help noticing how wanton she looked. Her hair, which was difficult to tame at the best of times, was totally tousled, her eyes sparkled above flushed cheeks and her lips looked so swollen they lent her mouth an insolent pout that was pure sex. Wow, she thought, transfixed for a moment by the sight, even *I* fancy me.

The thought made her giggle and she noticed the questioning look on Ivan's face as he reached out to caress her naked breasts. Rolling onto her side she pressed her breasts into his hands and stroked his hard cock. Her exploring fingers told her instantly that he had been circumcised. She could feel the smoothness of his shaft, with just the slightest ridge where her fingertips encountered a swollen vein and the taut bulb of his glans. As she stroked around the rim of his glans she heard him groan softly.

'That's a very light touch you have there,' he murmured hoarsely. His glance dropped to her mouth. 'I can't help wondering how your lips would feel on the same place.'

She smiled mischievously. 'Care to find out?'

Without waiting for his answer she scrambled down the bed. As she moved he quickly divested himself of his shoes, socks and trousers until he wore just a small pair of black Calvin Klein's, above which the top of his cock reared up.

'Very impressive,' she commented impishly, without making it clear whether she meant his designer label or his erection, 'but I think I'd prefer to see all of you.'

The black pants quickly joined the pile of clothing on the floor and in the meantime Danni pulled her dress off over her head and dumped it unceremoniously on top of the heap. Then, pressing her hand lightly but insistently against his chest, she pushed him back until he lay flat on the bed. Devoid of any restriction his cock reared up, a small, glistening tear of pre-emission emerging from the tip of its bulbous head.

Kneeling between his spread thighs, Danni leaned forward, her palms positioned either side of his hips to take her weight, and flicked out her tongue to lap up the drop of viscous fluid. She was gratified to hear Ivan groan with pleasure as she flicked her tongue experimentally around his glans and then slid her wet lips up and down his rigid shaft. If there was one thing she knew she was good at, it was giving oral pleasure. Her only hope was that he would not be like Tam and decline to give her the same in return.

Just thinking that he might actually treat her to the indulgence she truly craved sent her soaring to even greater heights of eroticism. Grasping the base of his cock with one hand she covered his glans with her lips, feeding more and more of his delicious length into her mouth until she engulfed him entirely. Then she sucked just a little harder as she slid her lips up and down his shaft.

She felt the slight tug on her hair as his hands delved into the silky mass, urging her mouth lower. A moment later, as she continued to lick and suck with increasing fervour, one hand left her hair and slid over her shoulder and down to cup her dangling breast. She gasped as Ivan's fingers pinched her nipple. Then he rolled the sensitive bud between finger and thumb, sending frissons of delicious pleasure coursing through her.

The blissful sensation of pure lust swamped her as she felt his cock expand within the wet cavern of her mouth. She could sense the excitement surging through him, feel the blood pumping beneath the fragile covering of his tautly stretched skin. A moment later a warm jet of salty fluid spurted into her mouth. Although she swallowed as quickly as she could a small amount escaped her lips and dribbled down her chin. Sitting back on her heels she wiped away the glutinous trail with the back of her hand, all the time smiling at him and feeling flushed with pleasure.

She couldn't help noticing how blissful his expression was. His eyes were heavy-lidded as he gazed back at her, his body relaxed, one lean, lightly tanned leg bent at the knee. At the apex of his thighs, his cock, still erect although not looking quite as rampant as before, jutted from a well-trimmed nest of silky hair. His scrotum looked loose and heavy, the skin dark and wrinkled in comparison to the smooth hairlessness of his upper thighs.

'You're beautiful,' Danni breathed as she gazed at him in wonder. It was the first time she had ever considered a man to be more than merely hand-

78

some but in Ivan's case she felt *beautiful* was the only way to describe him. Not only was his lean physique achingly desirable but his face was arresting in its perfection. His lashes cast long shadows over finely sculpted cheekbones and just beneath them she could make out the fiery glitter of his sapphire eyes.

'No, *you're* beautiful,' he insisted, stretching out a hand to her. 'Come here.'

Leaning forward again she moved up until she was lying full length on top of him. She could feel her breasts pressing into his chest and his cock nudging her belly. A sigh of pleasure escaped her lips as he cupped the back of her head and pulled her face close to his for a deep, searching kiss. At the same time his other hand stroked her shoulders for a moment before following the length of her spine and curving over the swell of her buttocks. While he continued to kiss her he stroked her bottom, occasionally sliding his fingers between her legs to tantalise the sensitive folds of her blossoming sex.

Feeling a renewed warmth, she squirmed against him, her breath hot against his ear as she told him how aroused she was feeling.

'As if I couldn't already tell,' he said lightly as he slid a couple of fingers inside her hungry sex and scissored them insolently. 'I think it's your turn for some pleasure now.'

Chapter Five

HARDLY DARING TO hope for too much, Danni allowed Ivan to roll her over on her back. He kept his fingers inside her as he moved and with his other hand patted her thigh.

'Bend your knees, darling,' he murmured. 'That's right, open your legs wide. I want to see all of you.'

Whimpering with barely contained longing, Danni complied with his request. She felt a flush of embarrassment mingled with lust suffuse her entire body as she watched him spread her labia wide open.

'Wonderful,' he said, 'so ripe and juicy.' Glancing at her face, he licked his lips suggestively. 'With such a succulent banquet on offer, I must sample it.'

Danni felt her stomach clench at the promise underlying his words and as he lowered his head between her open thighs, she found herself holding her breath. The first touch of his lips on her inner thigh was magnificent. So tormenting in its delicacy was it that she let the breath out of her lungs on a long gasp of pleasure. For what seemed like an eternity, he continued to kiss and nibble at the soft flesh of her thighs, while the silky ends of his hair whispering across her belly and the delicate flesh of her vulva tantalised her even more.

Panting with arousal, she had no option but to allow her body to cede to the demands of his mouth. Fire licked at her from the inside, while his tongue lapped delicately at her swollen folds and flicked insolently over her clitoris. As he drew back the tiny hood of flesh that concealed the sensitive tip of her clitoris and touched it with the end of his tongue she cried out, unable to bear the exquisite torment. The dark velvet cloak of eroticism descended over her, shrouding her naked body with ill-concealed passion.

'Oh, yes. Oh, God, yes!' she moaned hoarsely as the delicious thrill of orgasm overtook her.

It burned its way through her lower body, encouraging her to writhe her hips in the agony of ecstasy. With her arms stretched wide she clutched mindlessly at the bedspread, crumpling the pristine cotton into her palms. The waves of pleasure did not peak and abate instantly, but continued. Pressing the soles of her feet into the bed she opened her legs as wide as they would go and raised her hips, urging her desperate sex against the lush, warm wetness of Ivan's mouth.

He obliged her as she instinctively knew he would, cupping her buttocks in his hands and drawing every last ounce of pleasure from her body with his lips and tongue. When at last she felt the final tremors of her multiple climax ripple through her and dissolve, all the tension seemed to leave her body. With no strength left in them, her legs sprawled carelessly on the coverlet. Her arms felt limp and lifeless, the whole of her body as languid and amorphous as melted ice cream.

'Another time I will make love to you properly,' Ivan whispered to her, 'but not tonight.'

As she started to protest, although feebly, he added, 'It is already so late and we have to be up early in the morning. Or rather today.' He glanced at his wristwatch then turned his arm and held it to her face. 'See, it is already past two o'clock.'

That late! her mind registered with some shock, wondering how the time could have passed so quickly. She nodded weakly, ceding readily to the belief that he knew what was best for her.

'Eight o'clock at the latest for breakfast,' he told her as he rose from the bed and began pulling on his clothes. 'No slacking now, especially not on your first full day. Fauve will never forgive me otherwise.'

'OK,' she murmured tiredly, 'I'll be there.'

Just before he left he bent to kiss her one last time. As he did so Danni couldn't help noticing the sweet honeyed taste of her own juices on his lips. Around his mouth the skin, which was darkly shadowed with stubble, glistened with her moisture. Smiling, she reached up and rubbed her fingers over it.

'Can't have you leaving here looking like the cat

that's just got the cream,' she said, chuckling softly at the image.

He smiled back at her then, his eyes still dark and heavy-lidded with latent desire. 'Really?' he asked, 'Why not? Everyone will simply recognise that I have been a very lucky man tonight.'

Glowing inside at his compliment, Danni waved feebly to him as he left through the French window, drawing it closed behind him. For a few moments she simply lay where he left her, luxuriating in the unfamiliar sensation of feeling totally replete. Then, as she felt her heated body cooling in the night air, she crawled up to the top of the bed and slipped under the comforting warmth of the quilt.

She was asleep within moments of her head sinking into the pillow.

The next day dawned too quickly for Danni at first. Then, when she realised where she was and recollected the events of the previous evening, she suddenly felt a renewed vigour. Throwing off the quilt she sprang from the bed and enjoyed the powerful jets of warm water from the shower for a few minutes until she felt fully awake. Afterwards she wrapped her hair and body in towels and went back into the bedroom where she pondered her meagre selection of clothing.

Just as she was trying to decide whether she would be better off wearing shorts or leggings there was a knock at the door. Thinking it would be Ivan, Danni flung the door open and was surprised to see the diminutive figure of Fauve standing on the threshold.

'Oh,' Danni exclaimed, clutching the towel tighter around her.

'Do not bother to explain yourself, *chérie*,' Fauve interrupted as she walked boldly past Danni into the room. 'You thought I would be Ivan, no?'

Danni had the grace to blush.

'Well, no matter,' Fauve continued with a slight touch of imperiousness, 'I just come to give you this.' From behind her back she produced a leotard. Made of stretch fabric with a satiny sheen, it had short sleeves and consisted of horizontal stripes of pale blue and pink.

For a moment Danni felt lost for words as she took the garment from Fauve. 'It's, er, lovely,' she murmured as she found herself wondering how on earth she was going to fit all of her into it, 'but I'm not all that sure if it is my size.' She tried in vain to find a label.

'Then try it on, my pet,' Fauve said reasonably as she sat down on the end of the bed.

Danni hesitated, wondering if she should go into the bathroom to change. The last thing she really wanted to do was reveal her naked body with all its imperfections to Fauve's critical gaze. Nor give the chic Frenchwoman the benefit of watching her wrestle with the tiny garment. However, Fauve looked as though she had made herself comfortable and Danni felt rooted to the spot by indecision.

'Come on, *chérie*.' Fauve urged, 'we 'ave not the

84

whole day. Even as we speak, our *croissants* they go cold.'

With a mental shrug, followed by a physical one, Danni allowed the towel she was wearing to fall to the floor. She was startled when she heard the sharp clap of Fauve's hands.

'Ah, my dear, what a *fantastique* figure,' the Frenchwoman exclaimed. Temporarily struck dumb, Danni just stood there and watched as Fauve stood up and walked over to her. The older woman wandered around Danni, appraising her body thoroughly and dispassionately, as though she were a mannequin in a shop window. Then she smiled warmly. 'Such hips,' she enthused, 'such a lovely round bottom.' Danni flinched as Fauve's hand stroked across her buttocks. 'Oh, and those breasts, they are *magnifique*.'

Worried that Fauve was about to touch those as well, Danni stumbled back and mumbled something about having to hurry. Bending forward she stepped into the leotard and was surprised to find how easily it slipped up her body. Still, she felt quite red-faced when she straightened up and slipped her arms into the short sleeves. When she was standing upright she realised how high the leotard was cut on the legs. Glancing down she couldn't help noticing that a generous amount of curly hair was visible either side of the deep vee that just about covered her pubis.

'I'll need to get my bikini line done before I can wear this,' she mused aloud.

To her discomfort, Fauve squatted down in front

85

of her and stroked the curls absently. 'Do you have a razor?' she asked, glancing up at Danni's face, which now glowed an even brighter crimson.

'A – a Ladyshave,' Danni muttered, 'in the bathroom.' As she paused to glance over her shoulder Fauve sprang to her feet.

'*Un moment*,' she said, 'I will fetch it.'

While Fauve was in the bathroom, Danni – still feeling shaky by what had just transpired – turned to look at herself in the mirror. She was surprised and pleased to note how flattering the leotard was to her figure. Somehow it seemed to emphasise the good points about her shape, namely the high roundness of her breasts and the way her waist curved in then flared out sharply again at the hips. Even her legs looked longer and more shapely. Just as she was straining to look over her shoulder to see what her bottom looked like, Fauve came back into the room brandishing the little battery-operated razor.

'*Bon*,' she said, 'we soon make you as smooth as a baby's bottom, no?' Chuckling softly she squatted down in front of Danni again and flicked the switch on the shaver.

'Oh, no, I can do it,' Danni exclaimed quickly, trying to grab the shaver from Fauve's hand.

'Shush,' the Frenchwoman said, swatting Danni's hand away as though it were a fly, 'you cannot see properly to do it. Allow me.'

Opening her mouth to protest, Danni closed it again just as quickly. What was the point? she thought. Although she was small, Fauve was certainly a force to be reckoned with. There was little to be gained by arguing. All the same, she couldn't help feeling horribly embarrassed as Fauve began to stroke the head of the shaver over her curly thatch. When she thought Fauve was finished, Danni made to walk away but the Frenchwoman stopped her with a firm hand on her upper thigh.

'A second shaving is most important,' she said, ' 'ere, feel how the skin is still a little, er—' With a typically Gallic shrug she gave Danni a questioning look.

'Bristly?' Danni suggested, touching the places that Fauve's fingertips had skimmed over.

A smile lit up Fauve's delicate face. 'Yes, bristly,' she said. She gave Danni a look of apology. 'Five years I am in your country and still I do not speak perfect English.'

'Oh, but you do,' Danni insisted, forgetting her embarrassing predicament for a moment, 'and you put me to shame, honestly. I can hardly understand a word of any other language.'

'You are too kind,' Fauve said, continuing to smile. 'Perhaps I teach you a little French while you are 'ere, yes?'

'That's nice of you to offer,' Danni replied with a sheepish smile, 'but I'm far too slow to learn another language. I just can't seem to get the hang of it.'

Fauve made a tutting sound and looked disbelieving. Then she said, 'You must not describe yourself as slow, *ma chérie*, you are beautiful and no doubt talented in other areas.'

'Well, if that's the case I don't know what they are,' Danni laughed. 'All I seem to do is manage to make a mess of things. Even last night at dinner—' She allowed her words to trail away, remembering her rude outburst.

'Ah, last night,' Fauve said, applying the shaver to Danni's almost smooth skin once again. 'We were most disappointed you went to bed early. Meah especially.'

'Why Meah?' Danni asked, feeling confused. As far as she could remember, all the young Mauritian woman had done the night before was serve the food. They hadn't even spoken to each other.

A secretive smile touched Fauve's lips. 'That girl, she provide some very good entertainment. Last night was *formidable*. So good that tonight she will serve our meal again. But this time you will stay, no?'

'Oh, yes,' Danni said, nodding enthusiastically. She couldn't help wondering what sort of entertainment Meah provided. Perhaps she was a singer or played the guitar or something.

'That is good,' Fauve replied, interrupting her thoughts. 'We, that is to say, Ivan and I, want you to get the most enjoyment from your stay 'ere.'

'Well, that's very kind of you,' Danni began. She broke off as Fauve switched off the shaver and began stroking her fingertips across the areas of smooth skin either side of her groin. 'All done now?' she forced herself to ask lightly.

She wanted to take a step back, to get away from

the feather-light caresses that, to her discomfort, felt extremely tantalising. No other woman had ever touched that part of her body before. Chaste kisses on the cheek and the occasional hug by a good friend was all she had ever experienced. And all she had ever wanted to experience.

'Gosh, I'm starving,' Danni said, moving purposefully away, 'and I really ought to comb my hair through before it dries into tangles.'

'*Mais oui*,' Fauve agreed, appearing unconcerned as she straightened up and put the shaver on the dressing-table. 'Breakfast is always served in the kitchen – you know where that is, *n'est-ce pas*?'

'Yes.' Danni nodded and unwrapped the towel from her hair. 'I shouldn't be long.'

She watched Fauve cross the room to the door and in a moment, the petite Frenchwoman was gone. Only then did Danni feel her body sag with relief.

The kitchen was deserted when Danni wandered into it about ten minutes later. Her hair was still slightly damp but looked clean and healthy as it tumbled over her shoulders in thick tawny waves. To keep her warm in the cool farmhouse and to protect her modesty, she had pulled on a pair of black leggings and a baggy cream sweatshirt over the leotard. She hoped there would not be too many people present in the circus tent when she took them off for her first lesson. The garment, although flattering, was still far too skimpy and revealing for her liking.

The pine clock on the kitchen wall showed it was almost eight o'clock already and so she abandoned her idea of a leisurely breakfast. Instead, she quickly gobbled down a delicious *pain au chocolat*, spurning the idea of a second one and settling for a banana instead. Then she washed her breakfast down with half a mug of lukewarm filter coffee.

At just a few minutes past eight, Ivan appeared at the back door. As usual he looked gorgeous, Danni thought. Today he was dressed in a pair of black athletics shorts and matching vest. Although simple, the outfit set off his tanned skin and lean physique magnificently. She wondered if he would make any comment about the night before but her hopes were quickly dashed when he rubbed his hands together briskly and asked her if she was ready to get started.

'As ready as I'll ever be,' she said, standing up. She noticed he was regarding her quizzically. 'What's the matter?' she added when he didn't say anything.

'I thought Fauve was going to find a costume for you to wear,' he said. Then he shrugged, much in the same way as Fauve had done earlier, Danni noticed. 'Ah, well, it doesn't matter.'

'She did,' Danni said, following him to the door. 'I'm wearing it underneath.'

All at once Ivan smiled at her over his shoulder and she felt her breath catch at the warmth which enveloped her instantly. To her surprise and pleasure he stopped and put out his hand. Then he stroked her hair softly and cupped her chin, forcing her to meet the full impact of his gaze. Her knees felt weak and she gripped his wrist to steady herself.

'I forgot to mention – you were superb last night,' Ivan said softly as the pad of his thumb brushed over her lips. 'You are beautiful and thoroughly enjoyable.'

The effect of his words was cataclysmic. Immediately, Danni felt like ripping off her clothes and throwing him down on the kitchen floor. Instead she opened her mouth and drew in his thumb, sucking on it suggestively as her gaze remained locked with his.

Much to Danni's dismay, the 'Big Top' was already a hive of activity when she and Ivan arrived. There were quite a number of people she didn't recognise: some juggling and performing gymnastics, a couple swinging backwards and forwards on the trapeze, and a tall young man with fiery red hair, swallowing a long sword, the broad flashing blade of which he then withdrew with a flourish.

'How on earth does he do that?' Danni asked, wide-eyed.

'Relaxation of the throat,' Ivan replied simply. 'You should be good at it. I've been told it's like going down on a man.'

Danni blushed deeply, recalling the previous night and how delicious Ivan's cock had felt in her mouth.

'Well, I might give it a go then,' she said when she could speak again.

Ivan's brisk handclap shattered her reverie. 'Let's go over there and find out what else you can do already,' he suggested. He led her to one side of the circus ring where several padded mats were laid out next to each other on the floor to form a brightly coloured patchwork. 'How are you at gymnastics?' he asked.

Danni shrugged. 'I used to be able to turn cartwheels and do handstands when I was about ten years old,' she said. 'Other than that . . .'

Ivan brushed aside her doubts. 'Well, take those heavy clothes off and let's see if you can still do them,' he suggested.

Self-conscious, Danni pulled off the sweatshirt and leggings. When she straightened up she noticed Ivan was looking at her in much the same way Fauve had earlier.

'Do I look OK?' she asked tentatively as she pulled at the tight elastic that gripped her bottom and clung to her hips and groin.

'No,' Ivan said to her surprise. Then a smile lit up his face, the outer edges of his sparkling blue eyes crinkling. 'You do not look OK, Danni, you look fabulous. What a lucky man I was last night. And will be again, I hope.'

'Oh, you will,' Danni assured him, feeling her passion for him soar all over again. In a fit of elation she skipped across the layer of mats and executed three perfect cartwheels in a row. She straightened up, arms held out straight to the sides, and bounced lightly on the balls of her feet. 'I can still do them!' she cried, feeling flushed with success.

As Ivan gazed at her, noticing her bright pink cheeks, her tumbling hair and the way her breasts bounced as she moved, he had difficulty reminding himself that she was a grown woman and not a particularly precocious child. She brought out the masterful streak in him and seemed to delight in it, he recalled, thinking of the night before. When he had gone back to his room, he regretted that he had not stayed and made love to her completely. But that was just one night, he reminded himself – there were plenty of others to look forward to.

'OK, Danni,' he commanded briskly, turning his attention back to the present, 'how about those handstands you mentioned.'

To Danni's chagrin, she wasn't able to balance on her hands as easily as she had as a child. However, Ivan was patient with her and held her legs lightly until it became easier to keep her balance for longer periods of time. Finally she fell to the mats, feeling red-faced and short of breath.

'I'm knackered already,' she said, smiling up at Ivan.

'Knackered?' he asked. He squatted down beside her, his leg muscles bulging as he did so. Feeling tempted, Danni put her hand on his thigh and stroked it. His skin felt satin-smooth, the colour and texture reminding her of Belgian chocolate.

'Old English expression – you must have heard of it,' Danni said with a chuckle. 'I also feel starving again.'

Ivan laughed. 'My, my, you are a greedy thing, aren't you? Food and sex, is that all you think about?'

'I do now,' Danni replied pertly.

By lunchtime she had managed to accomplish a perfect sequence of tumbles. Under Ivan's careful instruction she learned how to perform backflips and couldn't believe how truly circus-like she felt. Sitting cross-legged on the mats she asked Ivan what other things he might teach her during her stay.

'That depends on what interests you,' he replied, 'and what is practical. Some things you cannot master in a matter of weeks.' He leaned forward and patted Danni's knee, trying not to allow his gaze to stray too obviously to her groin. When he had happened to glance there, he couldn't help noticing how the lips of her sex bulged enticingly under the tightly stretched material of her leotard. 'Let me see,' he continued. 'Can you ride a horse?'

'Sort of,' Danni said. 'I haven't ridden for a couple of years.'

'How about lion-taming?' he asked while forcing himself to keep a straight face.

Danni's eyes widened. 'Really?' she gasped. 'Do you have lions here?'

Laughing gently, he shook his head. 'No, not really,' he admitted. 'I was just teasing.'

'Pig,' she said with a broad grin. 'I always fancied having a go at that as a matter of fact. Mind you,' she added, leaning forward conspiratorially and deliberately treating Ivan to a good view of her cleavage, 'I've always wanted to be a ring-master.'

'Ah, that you cannot do,' Ivan said firmly.

Danni felt intrigued by his swift reply. 'Why not?'

He smiled. 'Because that is my job,' he said, 'I enjoy cracking the whip.'

Danni sat back and regarded him thoughtfully. I'll bet you do, she mused, surprised to feel a small quiver of excitement inside her. All at once she found herself wondering if her food had been doctored in some way, or if there was some kind of stimulant in the drinking water here at the farm. Her appetite for sex now seemed to be matched by a sudden interest in *kinky* sex. Feeling herself blush, she got quickly to her feet.

'Shouldn't we go and get some lunch now?' she said briskly as she glanced around the empty marquee. 'I can't help noticing the others went ages ago.'

Lunch was light, just salad, granary bread and fruit, although Ivan pointed out how sluggish they would all feel if they ate anything heavier.

'You may indulge yourself properly tonight at dinner,' he promised.

'It doesn't matter,' Danni said, patting her stomach and thinking how empty it still felt. 'I could do with losing some weight.'

Ivan's response was gratifying in its immediacy.

'No, you are lovely just the way you are. You wouldn't be Danni without all those delicious curves.'

Danni felt herself blushing and wondered if her inability to take a compliment was something she would ever grow out of. 'You're too kind,' she murmured, echoing Fauve's words earlier that day.

'No,' he said, taking her hand to lead her back to the circus tent, 'not kind, just truthful.'

Before their afternoon session began, Ivan asked Danni about some of the things she hoped to accomplish during her stay.

Impulsively, she said, 'Lots of things, but I've got a real urge to be able to ride a unicycle.'

She didn't know where the idea had suddenly come from. No doubt it was something she'd had locked away in her psyche since childhood, she realised. Glancing up at Ivan, she followed his movements with her eyes as he stood up and brushed away the few strands of straw that clung to his nicely rounded behind.

'No problem,' he said. 'Just give me a moment to get the necessary equipment, then I will teach you.'

He returned within moments, carrying a silver-framed unicycle with a black leather-covered seat.

'Here,' he said as he handed it to her, 'a bicycle made for one.' He paused and craned his neck to look around her. Then his face broke into a broad, crinkling smile. 'I really envy that saddle, knowing it's going to have your delicious behind resting on it.'

Danni's only comment was to blush profusely. He flattered her dreadfully but somehow always managed to sound completely sincere. Resting the unicycle against the blocks that edged the ring, she slipped off the elastic band which she wore around her wrist.

Scraping her hair into a high ponytail, Danni turned back to look at Ivan. She couldn't help noticing that he was staring at her with an odd expression that was halfway between amusement and desire.

'What's the matter?' she asked, trying to ignore the tightness in her chest.

To her relief he laughed aloud as he shook his head. 'Nothing,' he declared, grasping her lightly by the shoulders and gazing down at her. 'Only that you look about sixteen years old with your hair like that.'

She fluttered her eyelashes and pouted her lips coquettishly. 'Am I right in thinking you fancy me as a schoolgirl?' Glancing down to his groin, she was certain she could detect a certain tumescence there she hadn't noticed before.

'Don't tempt me like that, it's not fair,' Ivan said with a groan. 'I fancy you, as you put it, regardless of how you wear your hair. But right now I could—'

'Yes?' Danni butted in hopefully.

Instead, Ivan seemed to pull himself together. 'I could teach you how to ride the unicycle,' he said. 'Now hop on. I'll hold it steady for you.'

Steadying herself with a hand on Ivan's arm,

Danni climbed awkwardly onto the saddle. Even though Ivan was holding the back of the saddle firmly with one hand, the unicycle wobbled the moment she took her feet off the ground.

'I don't know if I'm going to be able to do this,' she said doubtfully. 'Like everything else, it's obviously harder than it looks.'

'You can ride an ordinary bicycle, can't you?' Ivan said over her shoulder.

'Yes, but this is a lot different,' she countered. 'There's a wheel missing for a start.'

'Just start pedalling,' he suggested. 'Even if you do fall off you won't hurt yourself on all this sawdust. Use your arms for balancing.'

'Like this?' Danni spread her arms out gingerly, wobbling the whole time.

'Perfect,' Ivan said encouragingly. 'Now, just pedal.'

Working her legs slowly at first, Danni started to pedal around the edge of the ring with Ivan running behind her still holding the saddle. Gradually, as she became more confident, she found her legs pistoning up and down, her speed becoming faster and faster. She used the gap in the ring wall as her marker and when she had done a second fast circuit she suddenly became aware that Ivan was standing a little way off, just watching her, with his hands on his hips. Immediately, she stopped pedalling and came to a wobbly halt. Putting down one foot to balance herself, she slid off the unicycle.

'I did it,' she cried, her face glowing with

triumph. 'I really did it, first go.'

She noticed Ivan looked as pleased as she felt and right at that moment what she most wanted to do was fling her arms around him and hug him half to death.

'Yes, you did,' he said as he planted a benevolent kiss on the top of her head. 'But you have to keep practising in order to be perfect.'

Two hours later, Danni felt as though she never wanted to ride the unicycle ever again for the rest her life. Her neck was stiff and aching, similarly her behind and her leg muscles were screaming from unaccustomed use. Also, she felt very thirsty.

'I've had it,' she complained, rubbing her saddle-sore backside. 'Could we get something to drink?'

He glanced at his watch as Danni bent forward and began to massage her thighs. 'I think we can call it a day,' he said. 'You've worked hard. I'm very proud of you.'

Although he made her feel the age he claimed she looked, Danni still felt extraordinarily pleased – and relieved that lessons were over for the day. Right at that moment she ached all over. The handstands and cartwheels she had done earlier that day had taken their toll on her body as well.

'I'm so unfit!' she wailed as she shuffled beside him back to the farmhouse. Her legs were stiffening up and there was a burning ache in her lower back.

'You'll get used to it,' Ivan said, without a hint of compassion. Then he glanced at her and added, 'I really meant what I said back there. You're proving to be an excellent pupil.'

'Well, thanks,' Danni said, trying not to look too pleased. 'Now all this excellent pupil needs is a long cold drink, a warm bath and about ten hours sleep.'

Smiling at her, Ivan glanced at the kitchen clock. 'Four hours maximum,' he said. 'Fauve wants to eat early tonight. I understand she has plans.'

Although she thought this sounded mysterious, Danni hadn't the energy to pursue the conversation. After a long drink of fresh lemonade, she made her way back to her room, bathed away her aches and pains, then fell into a deep, dreamless sleep.

Chapter Six

REVIVED BY HER sleep, Danni got up and slipped on her only other dress – loose yellow cheesecloth with buttons down the front from the deeply scooped neckline to the ankle-skimming hem. She felt a tingle of anticipation as she dressed, wondering what might happen after dinner. Hoping the evening would end up in bed with Ivan again, she switched on the bedside lamps in readiness and added judicious squirts of perfume to every erogenous zone. Satisfied that she was ready at last, she made her way to the inappropriately named Great Hall.

The same people were gathered there again: Lettie and Rose were seated either side of Randi, with Ivan next to Lettie, then Fauve on the other side of him. The only free seat was between Aldous and Guido. As Danni sat down she flashed a smile across the table at Ivan, wishing he wasn't seated quite so far away from her. The power of the smile he gave her in return nearly knocked her backwards. He was dressed in a black shirt and trousers and his hair seemed even whiter, his eyes even bluer and his skin even more tanned in contrast.

By way of a change, Fauve had ditched her usual black clothing in favour of red – a short silk shift worn with matching high-heeled sandals. Matte lipstick of exactly the same colour made her small mouth look lush and pouting. Danni felt an irrational stab of jealousy as she eyed the other woman surreptitiously. If it wasn't bad enough that she looked so chic and sexy and vibrant, she was also seated where Danni would like to be – next to Ivan – and kept touching him every other minute, it seemed.

Right now, Fauve's hand rested lightly on Ivan's shoulder and her face was animated as she leaned across him to talk to Lettie.

A moment later, Danni's disturbing thoughts were interrupted by a deep voice with an American accent.

'You look lovely tonight. Like a daffodil in full bloom.'

Danni started in surprise at the unexpected compliment. She had been so enthralled by watching Fauve's movements that everyone else in the room, apart from Ivan of course, was temporarily forgotten.

'I, oh, thank you. Thank you very much,' she gasped as she turned her head.

It was Aldous who had spoken and the first thing that struck Danni as she looked at him was the brilliance of his smile. Full pink lips stretched wide over a perfect set of teeth, the whiteness of which seemed startling against the olive canvas of his complexion. Like Ivan, he had long hair that reached past his shoulders, but his was dark and curly. She seemed to recall Ivan mentioning that Aldous was a New York Italian, which would explain both the accent and the Latin looks.

'Don't mention it,' he said reaching for his glass of wine. He paused to sip it then asked, 'How did your first day go? I saw you tumbling on the mats this morning – very impressive.'

Danni blushed and, grabbing her own glass, gulped at the wine hastily. The way he spoke made her wonder if it was her acrobatic skills he found impressive, or the sight of her jumping about in her skimpy leotard.

'Ivan's a good teacher,' she murmured.

He grinned broadly then and squeezed her upper arm lightly. 'Ah, but it's the quality of the raw material that really counts.' He leaned back and appraised Danni blatantly, in a way that made her feel instantly defensive. She wanted to wrap her arms around her body but steeled herself to resist the temptation. After a moment, Aldous nodded appreciatively. 'I'd say the raw material looks pretty damn good from where I'm sitting.'

'Thanks,' she said again, not knowing what else to say.

She cursed herself inwardly for not being sophisticated enough to accept a compliment graciously and for being unable to indulge in witty repartee. Glancing across the table she noticed that Fauve obviously had the talent she so badly lacked. The Frenchwoman had nearly everyone else in her thrall and Ivan was laughing openly and smiling at her in a way that was so intimate it made Danni's chest ache to see it.

'Fauve and Ivan are old friends,' Aldous said, following Danni's gaze.

'So I understand,' Danni answered before taking another large gulp of her wine. This evening it was a dry, crisp white. 'Have they always run the circus school together, do you know?'

'Yes, I think so.' Aldous nodded. 'As far as I understand it, they have worked together all over the world. Ivan's knife-throwing act is internationally famed but now he prefers the role of ringmaster.'

'Yes, he told me,' Danni said. 'And what about you – what do you do?'

He shrugged. 'Juggle, tame lions, walk the tightrope . . . A bit of everything really.'

Danni smiled. 'There are no lions here, are there?' she asked, already knowing the answer.

'No way,' he said, 'but jeez, there are a bundle of other things for me to do around here. Plus I handle all the choreography.'

'Choreography – what for?' Danni asked.

'The shows,' Aldous replied, giving her a vaguely curious look. 'Every special show is choreographed. They are more like modern ballet than circus performances. Artistic – you know. Basically, the movements need to be smooth and sequential.

And erotic, of course.'

Danni felt her stomach do a backflip of its own. 'In what way do you mean erotic?' She was surprised when Aldous made a sort of growling noise. Then she saw he was laughing.

'I can't believe you just asked that,' he said. When he saw that Danni's blank look meant she truly didn't understand, he added, 'What do you think *Cirque Erotique* means?'

'I don't know,' Danni began, but immediately comprehension dawned and she added, 'Although I think I'm just beginning to get the picture.' Swallowing the rest of her wine she nodded as Aldous picked up the bottle and made to refill her glass. 'Thanks,' she muttered. She took another gulp just to calm her churning stomach, then said, 'Do I take it that everyone involved does – well – erotic things as part of the performance?'

'Got it in one, sweetpea,' Aldous said.

Despite her growing anxiety, Danni couldn't help asking, 'What sort of things?'

'Sensual things,' he replied. 'Caressing, stroking, generally giving each other pleasure. Then there's a grand finale where everyone gets involved with everyone else.'

'In front of an audience?' Danni asked, unable to believe what she was hearing. The quick shake of his head that she was hoping for didn't materialise. Instead, to her dismay, he nodded.

'Oh, don't worry,' he said airily. 'The audience don't walk in off the streets. They're all carefully vetted by Fauve and Ivan. Some of them travel thousands of miles just to see the spectacle.'

Danni felt as though her head was floating a long way above her shoulders. What Aldous was suggesting seemed like part of a bad dream. In a moment she would wake up and Ivan would be beside her, telling her that *Cirque Erotique* was simply an ordinary circus, just like any other.

With hope in her heart she glanced across the table at the man she so desperately needed to talk to. Unfortunately, he was deeply involved in a discussion with Randi. By the gestures he was making, it looked as though he were describing some sort of acrobatic sequence.

'OK, Aldous,' Danni said after fortifying herself with another gulp of wine, 'tell me what all the other people here do. And how come there were so many people in the circus tent today that aren't here tonight? I don't really understand the set-up.' She shifted uncomfortably in her seat as Aldous slipped his arm across the back of her chair.

He leaned towards her conspiratorially. 'First of all,' he said, 'call me Al. Second of all, everyone here is either instructing or being instructed by someone else.' He glanced across the table then back at Danni. 'Lettie is instructing Randi, Rose is instructing Guido and I am instructing Meah, who's just come back for the second time around. You know Ivan is your instructor, which just leaves Fauve to handle all the administration and stuff. She and Ivan take it in turns to instruct. It's always boy-girl you see.'

'And the others?' Danni prompted as she tried

106

to assimilate what Aldous, or rather Al, was telling her.

'Experienced performers, sweetpea,' he said. His arm moved from the back of the chair to drape lightly around her shoulders. 'They choose to live either on the farm, or outside in one of the surrounding villages.'

'And do they take part in the special performances?'

He smiled. 'Some, not all. It depends how many people are needed and if there is a broad enough range of skills. It is still a circus performance when all said and done, just with the erotic slant, that's all.'

That's all! Danni thought, wondering how quickly she could pack and get away from there. Her hopes for a wonderful couple of weeks had taken a nosedive. Wasn't it typical? Just when she'd finally got up the courage to do something entirely for herself. And found a man she really fancied . . .

When she glanced up she was surprised to see Ivan gazing at her across the table. He knows, she thought wildly, feeling stupid for believing he could read her mind, yet believing it all the same.

Feeling like a condemned woman, she ate a hearty meal. In all honesty, she thought as she speared a tiny Jersey potato with her fork, the food was too good to ignore. Tender spring lamb heavily flavoured with garlic was served with new potatoes cooked in their skins, a medley of wild mushrooms and a crisp green salad. She washed down the excellent meal with copious amounts of Chardonnay – having made a point of looking at the label on the bottle nearest to her, just so she knew exactly what she was getting drunk on.

All the way through the meal she was aware of Ivan's gaze upon her. He watched her cut her meat – the knife sliding through it like butter – raise her fork to her mouth, chew, swallow, sip some wine . . .

Don't keep looking at me, she willed him silently. Despite her best intentions her body seemed intent on betraying her. There was a warmth in her pelvis that was achingly familiar, as was the tiny pulse of her clitoris which beat insistently. There was no way of ignoring her body's responses to him. And no way of denying her intention to get him back into her bed that night.

There was something so sensuous about his gaze. Like a caress, it warmed and tantalised her body. She could feel it, like fingers, sliding under the flimsy lace of her bra and stroking her breasts. Down over her stomach it slithered, touching, teasing, energising her flesh. All her nerve endings were tingling. The moisture flowed freely from her body to soak the crotch of her cream satin and lace knickers. She closed her eyes trying to block out the image of his lambent gaze. Don't, she prayed silently again, don't just look at me, touch me . . .

The fingers stroking the nape of her neck came as a blessed relief. Was it Ivan? Turning her head she was surprised to see not the object of her desire but Fauve, looking secretive and excited all at once. Glancing back, Danni noticed that Ivan was still sitting across the table from her. Only he was no longer looking at her but in deep discussion with Guido. It shocked Danni to realise that she hadn't exchanged a single word with the nice young Italian, let alone noticed him move from her side.

Fauve took the seat that Guido had vacated. She smoothed her fingertips along the length of Danni's arm, the tips of her nails scraping lightly down the outside of Danni's breast.

'Ready for dessert?' the Frenchwoman asked.

Danni swallowed, feeling her throat go dry and her head swim. It wasn't just the wine having that effect on her, she realised with a jolt of surprise – she was actually enjoying Fauve's innocent caress. The Frenchwoman's light floral scent filled her nostrils and she was surprised to notice how easily she detected the faint undertone of feminine musk. Whether it was Fauve's or her own she couldn't be sure but the aroma tantalised her, flickering around the sensitive membranes of her nostrils and flooding her head.

Gradually, the smell of sex and the heat of it enveloped her.

'What is for dessert?' she managed to blurt out.

She couldn't help noticing how Fauve's liquid brown eyes darkened as she replied, 'The most succulent fruits imaginable.'

As if on cue, Meah reappeared. Danni glanced at her without surprise. It was though she knew all along what was about to happen and was party to all the secrets contained within the sensual philosophy of *Cirque Erotique*.

Looking even more exotic than the evening before, Meah's eyes sparkled and her full mouth glistened under a coat of plum-coloured lipstick. Expertly smudged kohl rimmed her almond-shaped eyes, making them seem even darker and more shadowed, above which her sable brows were plucked into fine arches. Glancing over the young woman, Danni couldn't help noticing how curvaceous her figure seemed in the black and white maid's uniform. The mass of white petticoats frothed over the tops of endless black-stockinged legs and the frilled neckline showed a generous amount of dusky cleavage. In contrast to her voluptuous appearance, her glossy dark hair was tonight pinned up in an elegant chignon and she wore a pair of diamanté earrings to match the collar encircling her slender throat.

'Over here, Meah,' Fauve ordered softly, crooking a finger.

The young woman seemed to glide across the room, her grace unimpeded by the four-inch black patent stilettoes she wore. Fauve moved her chair back from the table and turned it slightly, motioning for Danni to do the same. In the gap between them Meah stood motionless. Her demeanour was submissive as she clasped her hands in front of her and lowered her gaze.

Danni glanced at the young woman, then turned her attention to the other occupants of the room. The atmosphere was electric. Everyone seemed to be watching, waiting for something to happen. Erotic tension gripped her as she caught the flash of Ivan's smile. There was something knowing in his eyes and just the merest suggestion of assurance. It was as though his sultry gaze conveyed the message, 'Enjoy this for now but don't forget what you have to come later.'

All at once, Danni realised that being given licence to enjoy herself, to let herself go, was exactly what she needed. She wanted to please Ivan and please herself. There was nothing to fear. Even the unknown held a beguiling promise.

Tearing her gaze away from Ivan's with difficulty, Danni noticed that Fauve was stroking Meah's thigh. The Frenchwoman's fingernails – tonight painted a glossy red to match her outfit – skimmed lightly over the dark welt of stocking top and scratched the olive skin above. Up and down her fingertips travelled. It mesmerised Danni, who felt her own body responding as if it were she who was being touched.

'Raise your skirts,' Fauve murmured to Meah.

Danni felt her breath catch as, unhesitatingly but with provocative slowness, the young woman gathered the froth of petticoats in her slender hands and lifted the front of her dress.

A triangle of glossy dark hair showed. Perfectly trimmed, it concealed the womanly pouch of flesh beneath. Meah stood perfectly still as Fauve reached out and stroked the curls covering the young woman's mound. The red fingernails raked through them, pulling and parting.

Gradually Danni became aware that Meah was breathing heavily. Her eyes were heavy-lidded, she noticed as she glanced up at the young woman's face. And her plummy lips were wet and slightly parted.

Moving her hand away from Meah's pubis, Fauve patted her on the top of the thigh. 'Go and show the others, Meah,' she commanded gently. 'You know they're waiting.'

Dry-mouthed with anticipation, Danni watched the young woman move away. Still keeping her dress raised at the front, she walked around the back of Danni's chair and stood in front of Al.

'Lovely, sweetpea,' he said in an appreciative tone.

He slid the palm of his hand over her glossy thatch. Then his middle finger burrowed into it, sliding into the crevice between Meah's outer labia.

With a sense of disbelief at what she was witnessing, Danni watched his finger stroking up and down. Crossing her legs she clenched her thighs together, anxious to quell the dull throbbing of her clitoris. There was no need to draw her eyes away from the hypnotic movement of Al's finger to glance at Meah's face. She could feel the young woman's excitement. Heat mingled with erotic yearning emanated from her in waves. And the scent of her arousal was unmistakable.

Danni felt a rush of her own moisture and ached to put her hand between her legs. Her breasts swelled beneath the tight confines of her bra and she had difficulty in controlling her breathing. Putting up a hand to her forehead, she wiped away a few trickles of perspiration.

The next thing she knew, Ivan was by her side. Squatting down between Danni and Meah, he hardly glanced at the exotic young woman but turned his full attention to Danni.

'Feeling warm, darling?' he asked as he slid his hand along her leg, from hip to knee.

She looked down at his hand as it rested there and, involuntarily it seemed, her crossed legs slid apart. Almost in a trance, she watched as his fingers worked the material of her long dress up her leg to expose her bare thigh. Then his hand caressed her, squeezing and massaging the warm silky flesh he had uncovered.

'I, I—' Danni gasped, feeling lost for words.

'Don't fight it, darling,' he murmured. 'We're all friends here. Everyone just wants you to have a good time, however much or as little as that may mean.'

'I don't want to make a fool of myself again,' Danni admitted in a hoarse whisper.

Ivan resisted the urge to laugh, knowing that it would be inappropriate when Danni looked so bewildered. Coming to terms with one's own erotic desires was not something to be taken lightly. He remembered his own early experiences only too well and empathised completely with the lovely woman by his side.

'There is no right and wrong when it comes to sensual discovery,' he said gently. 'At least not among consenting adults. Wickedness is the denial of pleasure, not the exploration of it.'

'I wish I could believe that,' Danni answered.

Her cheeks felt flushed with shame and confusion. She noticed how Ivan's fingers had started to describe small circles on the inside of her thigh, just above her knee. His caress was so chaste and felt so achingly delicious that Danni wondered why she felt she should be stopping him. What if his hand moved higher up her thigh? she asked herself, would that make a difference? In her heart of hearts she knew it wouldn't. She trusted Ivan and felt confident that he wouldn't push her, or do anything which he knew would embarrass her in front of the others.

Danni's inner conflict was apparent on her face, Ivan noticed. Yet he sensed how her resolve not to enjoy herself was weakening.

'Just go with the flow, Danni,' he said. 'Don't push it but don't fight it either. Simply take each moment as it comes.' It was then he turned his head and glanced at Meah. 'Look at her,' he continued. 'I mean really look. Does she seem as though she's hating the attention she's receiving?'

Against her better judgement, Danni looked. To her surprise she noticed that Lettie had taken Al's seat and it was her hand that now caressed the dark triangle of curls. Fauve was standing behind Meah, stroking her throat below the diamanté collar. Meah's head was thrown back, touching Fauve's shoulder and the expression on her face was one of pure bliss.

A tight knot of erotic tension gripped Danni as she watched, enthralled. Fauve's hands slid lower, palms flat, her fingertips inching under the frilled neckline. Meah arched her back more and Danni could see Fauve's hands working beneath the black satin, her fingers flexing as she massaged Meah's breasts.

'Oh, God!' Danni heard the gasp and wondered for a moment where it came from. But as Ivan's grip intensified on her thigh and she heard him whisper, 'It's OK, Danni, just let yourself go,' she realised the exclamation had come from her own mouth.

She gazed at him, though her glazed eyes hardly registered his features. The temperature surrounding her seemed so warm all of a sudden that the thin dress she was wearing stuck to her and seemed like an encumbrance. With trembling fingers she unfastened the top couple of buttons and blew down the front of her dress.

Beside her she could hear Meah panting and whimpering. The young woman had spread her legs wider apart and now she was teetering on the high heels, her legs trembling so hard Danni could see the muscles quivering. Her pelvis was thrust forward, Lettie's fingers working between her legs.

'Let's see that naughty little clitoris, shall we?' Lettie murmured, parting Meah's outer labia.

To Danni, the intimate flesh thus exposed looked red and swollen, the folds glistening with Meah's own juices. The young woman shuddered as Lettie plunged a finger into the hungry wetness of her vagina and slicked another trail of moisture over her inner folds. She took care to coat the swelling bud of Meah's clitoris, Danni noticed, rubbing her finger around and over it in tight little circles.

Knowing how good it must feel, Danni sensed her own clitoris responding. She could feel her sex swelling and becoming wetter. The crotch of her knickers was saturated and she could feel her clitoris throbbing mercilessly. The temptation to grab Ivan's hand and put it between her legs was overwhelming. She turned to him with an anguished expression, hoping he could read the unspoken message in her eyes.

'Feeling a little horny, are we, sweetpea?' The runny-honey tones of Al's voice touched her ear and she noticed that Ivan was standing up, to be replaced by Al.

Not you, she wanted to cry, I want Ivan! But the object of her desire was already moving away, leaving her with a lascivious wink and the mouthed words, 'Later, darling.' Her body cried out to him not to leave her. It seemed cruel but she couldn't help wondering, in the next instant, if he was trying to tell her something. Perhaps he thought she was growing too dependent on him already.

Stop it! she told herself sharply, you are a grown woman with no ties. No one is here to judge you, why not just make the most of what's on offer? Realising she may never get an opportunity like this again, or at least not for a long time, she resolved to try and loosen up. Just to help ease her inhibitions she reached for her wine-glass.

'I'm not sure if I'm cut out for this kind of thing,' she admitted to Al, who was now squatting by her side where Ivan had been moments before.

He smiled warmly, his hand mirroring Ivan's caress on her thigh. 'Sure you are, sweetpea,' he assured her. 'Everyone is if they bother to explore their needs properly.'

She shook her head, noticing how fuzzy it felt. 'But that's the trouble, I don't know what my needs are. Not really.'

'Do you need an orgasm?' he asked, shocking her.

Danni knew her cheeks had turned pink. Full of shame, she nodded. Her breath caught as she felt his hand sliding over her thigh, delving under her dress.

'You're wet,' he commented, as if she didn't know. He put a finger to her lips as she opened her mouth to reply.

Moaning quietly, Danni felt his fingertips brushing her inner thigh. They touched the cream lace covering her mound and slid over the wet satin clinging to her crotch. The fingertips eased under the satin to stroke the blossoming lips of her sex. Groaning, Danni clutched at the edge of the table with one hand and with the other raised the wine-glass to her lips and tipped the contents down her throat.

She put the glass down shakily, wishing she could have a refill. Alcohol was not ideal but at that moment she would have been grateful for anything which could dull the burning waves of eroticism that were sweeping through her body. Her nipples felt as though they were on fire. They chafed uncomfortably against the cream lace of her bra and without thinking she tried to adjust it, pulling at the strip of satin which linked the cups. As she tugged, the front fastening sprang undone. The relief was exquisite. Her breasts felt liberated, though the hard buttons of her nipples now rubbed against the cheesecloth dress, their outline clearly visible through the thin fabric.

'Go with it, sweetpea,' Al urged as his fingers stroked her sex.

He reached down with his other hand and began unbuttoning her dress from the hem upwards.

Stop it! Danni wanted to cry out. Her hand fluttered to his wrist and tried ineffectually to stop him. Instead, she found her fingers moving away from his wrist and sliding over her belly to her groin. She could feel the movement and breadth of his fingertips under the damp scrap of satin as they stroked her clitoris and the rim of her vagina.

Her flesh seemed hypersensitive. The warmth and wetness emanating from the pouch of flesh between her legs was unmistakable. The tropical sensation of her arousal transmitted itself to her fingertips, encouraging her to slide her hand up over her torso to cup one of her breasts. Under the thin cotton she could feel its roundness and its weight. The nipple was hard and swollen, the sensitive bud becoming even more aroused as she rubbed her palm over it.

All at once, it seemed, her senses were alive and flooded with inspiration. Although Al's body partially blocked her view she could see that Meah was having a good time. With legs spread wide she was enjoying the oral attentions of Lettie, while Fauve had somehow released her breasts from the tight confines of her dress. Full and olive-skinned they filled the Frenchwoman's tiny hands, the nipples and surrounding areolae as sweetly enticing as chocolate buttons.

As she gazed at them Danni was surprised to feel a rush of desire. She wanted to take those nipples between her lips and lathe them with her tongue. Somehow she imagined that they would taste as delicious as they looked and she found herself longing to give another woman the sort of pleasure that she herself enjoyed.

To Danni's surprise, Rose came up behind her. The young woman's hands slid down the sides of Danni's neck to ease the loosened neckline of her dress over her shoulders. As the young woman caressed her bared shoulders Danni couldn't help marvelling at the delicacy of her touch. Light and feminine, Rose's fingers with their short rounded nails skimmed over the golden brown skin which lay like sculpted satin over the upper swell of Danni's breasts.

The whimper that escaped Danni's lips was unstoppable. She felt a tremendous surging excitement that at the same time seemed limitless. There was no rush to take her pleasure, she realised, relaxing further into the chair and spreading her legs wider. True sensuality had no respect for the passing of time.

Where do I get all these ideas? She wondered at that moment. Was it really the case that *Cirque Erotique* had already begun to work its magic on her? Could it happen that quickly, or was this merely an expression of her true desires? Desires that had, without her knowing it, been sublimated beneath the outer mantle of duty and the code of ethics that had been taught to her. Normal, wasn't that what she was? If so, what was normal?

A moment later Ivan came back to her. He stood by her right shoulder. Danni felt a sense of relief and watched as he bent over her. His breath was warm on her bare shoulder as he kissed it and lathed his tongue over her burning skin. Between her legs she could feel her vulva responding to Al's touch, her vagina welcoming the intrusion of his fingers eagerly, her clitoris swelling under the practised manipulation by his thumb.

'I'm proud of you, Danni,' Ivan murmured quietly to her, 'you seem to be really enjoying yourself.'

In answer, Danni moaned and arched her back. Touch me, her body screamed. Ivan, Al, Rose, anyone – just touch me!

Danni heard the harsh cry of Meah's orgasm and felt her own body respond. Her clitoris pulsed hard. Her vagina, wet and stretched wide open by Al's broad probing fingers, spasmed and grasped at the digits inside her. One breast was enfolded by the delicate softness of Rose's hand, the other by the familiar palm of Ivan. Unknown fingers plucked at the remaining buttons on her dress, the material drawn back to expose her scantily clad body. Her breasts were bared, her vulva only just concealed by the damp scrap of cream lace and satin.

Rose and Ivan took their hands away from her breasts simultaneously, each of them moving so that they could lean over her.

Glancing down through eyes heavy-lidded with arousal, Danni saw her own torso, curvaceous and golden brown. Her breasts looked full and ripe, the nipples swollen and hard like underripe cherries. The kneeling figure of Al was all but blocked out by Rose's slight frame but Danni could feel him. Oh God, could she feel him. He knew the workings of a woman's body, she realised as she felt the pad of his thumb caressing her clitoris in maddeningly tantalising circles.

The moment she felt her nipples being enclosed by the warm, sucking mouths of Rose and Ivan, Danni felt her body go into a spasm of lust. It oozed outwards from her solar plexus in continuous waves of warmth. Abandoning all shame, she cried out and ground her sex ardently against Al's fingers. A strong spear of heat shot up inside her and exploded. Behind her closed eyelids she saw white lights. Every part of her body seemed gripped in the poignancy of sensual abandon.

She came back down to earth shakily and with a

flutter of shame at having let herself go so easily.

'You are beautiful, *chérie*,' Fauve said, surprising Danni with a kiss on the cheek and a deft stroke of her elegant hand over Danni's left breast. She tweaked the stiff nipple and smiled warmly. 'Tomorrow night you will enjoy even more, yes?'

Tomorrow night? The prospect seemed tantalising. But there was still the rest of this night to consider and Danni hoped fervently that Ivan wouldn't assume that she was already satisfied.

She needn't have worried, she realised, as he bent to whisper salacious promises in her ear.

'Come,' he said, taking her hand and helping her to rise to her feet. 'I will take you back to your room.' Danni wobbled unsteadily as she stood up. With a docile air she waited as Ivan fastened her bra, wrapped her dress around her again and fastened most of the buttons. 'You'll do,' he said with a smile. He patted her bottom indulgently and took her hand again. Then he commanded softly, 'Bed, young lady.'

Chapter Seven

IN SHARP CONTRAST to the orgiastic nature of the evening, the couple of hours that Danni spent with Ivan afterwards were as intimate and seductive as they could possibly have been. And it came as no surprise to Danni that he turned out to be a incredible and tender lover.

He took his time to undress her, kissing every minute portion of her flesh as he exposed it. Then when he finally made love to her he did so gently, urging her to lie back on the bed before sliding smoothly into her.

She was so aroused that her body was a wet and willing vessel. As soon as she felt the delicious length of his cock enter her, she wrapped her legs around his waist and urged her pelvis to match him thrust for thrust.

As he moved inside her, he raised her arms over her head and pinned them there with one hand, his grip light but firm. It was this that disintegrated the last of Danni's inhibitions. Her last vestige of reserve turned to voluptuousness as she moved beneath him. To cede control to him was a delicious luxury. He would give her pleasure, *was* giving her pleasure, lots of it. If she learned nothing else during her stay at the circus school she would know from now on exactly how much of a sexual, sensual woman she was.

Sunlight streamed through the thin silk curtains at the bedroom window, casting a diffused golden light over its stark whiteness. Luxuriating in the warmth and the contentment she felt from her new experiences, Danni lay on her back and gazed up at the delicate canopy above her. This is not a dream, she told herself for the umpteenth time since she had woken up that morning. Incredible as it seems this is all real and this – she paused in her thoughts to stroke a hand voluptuously over her naked breasts – is the real me.

The coming day stretched out before her full of promise. She was going to ask Ivan if he would let her try the trapeze. The wonderful, confident feeling that enveloped her made her sure of her own capabilities. And if she proved to be a failure on the trapeze? Well, she would just try something else.

Instead of leaping from the bed with her usual exuberance, she slid gracefully from it. She intended to make a conscious effort to behave in a more sophisticated fashion. *Sensual woman* was her key phrase. The one that she hoped would eventually prove to be an apt description of her. Character traits such as *scatterbrained* and *impetuous* would now be anathema to her personality. She would be elegant. She would be serene. And above all, she would be supremely, sublimely erotic.

Skipping breakfast, she went straight to the marquee behind the farmhouse. There she found Rose, Lettie, Randi and Guido already hard at work. Lettie was teaching Randi how to juggle a set of brightly coloured hoops, while way above their heads Rose was shouting instructions to Guido who swung on the trapeze.

'Ready to work, little one?' Ivan said, coming to stand beside her.

Turning her head slowly – gracefully does it, she reminded herself – Danni smiled at him.

'As ready as I'll ever be.'

He stroked a finger along her arm. 'Sleep well?'

Her smile broadened. 'Like a top. And talking of big tops, I wouldn't mind having a go up there.'

Ivan followed her gaze to the small platform way up near the roof of the tent where Rose was waiting for Guido. As Danni and Ivan watched, the young Italian swung up to the platform and grasped the ladder rail. Rose caught the trapeze and secured it with a rope as Guido climbed off.

Danni noticed Ivan flash her a curious look. 'Are you sure you feel ready for that, Danni?' he asked, 'I don't want you to rush things and risk scaring yourself.'

'I'm not frightened,' she insisted. 'I'm dying to have a go.'

She was displaying more bravado than she felt.

Behind her ribs her heart was thumping and her stomach felt knotted up with anxiety just at the thought of climbing the ladder. Nevertheless, after Rose and Guido had descended, at Ivan's instruction she started to climb.

It was important to take it one step at a time and keep looking up, Danni told herself. She chuckled softly to herself. Somehow, it seemed an appropriate course of action for her to follow regardless of whether she was on the ladder or with both feet safely on the ground.

'Nearly there, Danni,' Ivan said encouragingly from below her.

Danni blushed when she realised what a wonderful view he must be getting. To her surprise, that morning she had discovered a small pile of freshly laundered clothes on her dressing-table. These included her leotard which, despite her missing breakfast, was still much too tight and revealing. Now she was aware of the way her bottom and hips bulged and was certain that the clinging fabric showed the outline of her vulva and the groove between her buttocks to perfection.

Unable to resist it, she called down, 'Enjoying the view?'

Ivan's deep, throaty chuckle was immediate. 'I'd be lying if I said I wasn't.'

When Danni finally reached the small platform she waited for Ivan to join her. Risking a glance down, she watched the top of his white-blond head rise up, closely followed by his shoulders and then the rest of him. Once again he was wearing black shorts and vest and looked superbly lean and athletic. Feeling the tightness in her stomach turn to melting warmth as she looked at him, she couldn't help putting a hand on his forearm. It was lightly furred with hair so fair it was almost invisible and the muscles were hard and well-defined beneath the toasted brown skin.

'Don't look down until you feel fully confident,' he told her.

Danni laughed nervously. 'I wasn't going to. I was just looking at you.'

Now she was up where she had wanted to be she wished she was back on the ground. The space separating their platform from the one on the other side of the ring seemed vast – unbridgeable.

Picking up a broad leather belt attached to an elasticated rope, Ivan told her to hold her arms out to the sides.

'You look worried,' he murmured gently. 'Here, let's put this on you. It should make you feel a lot more secure.'

She glanced at the band of brown leather and then up at his face. 'What is it?'

'A safety lunge,' he said, fastening the belt around her waist. 'Although the net would break your fall this is an additional precaution. It's especially useful for complete beginners.'

Feeling grateful to him, Danni stood obediently with her arms held out. As he put his arms around her to circle her waist with the belt she breathed in his special scent and luxuriated in the warmth and masculinity emanating from him.

'Could you imagine having sex up here?' she joked as she considered the improbability of achieving such a feat.

Ivan glanced at her face as he straightened up. A wolfish smile touched his lips and his blue eyes glittered. 'It *is* possible,' he said, sounding mysterious and full of promise all at once.

He's done it already! Danni realised straight away. To her surprise she found that she didn't feel any twinge of possessive jealousy, only curiosity. Not to mention excitement at the possibility of trying it for herself.

'Later then,' she said boldly, 'once I've got my bearings a bit.'

Ivan laughed and he slapped her buttocks lightly as he turned her around to face the trapeze. 'My, my, you are becoming adventurous,' he said.

'Of course,' Danni replied, tossing her head with feigned aplomb, 'I intend to become the original daring young woman on the flying trapeze.'

Ivan smiled. 'That wasn't what I meant.'

She was delighted when Ivan put his arms around her. He squeezed her waist, then slid the palm of one hand up her torso to cover her breast. He held her against him tightly, her back pressing against the hard wall of his body. Danni sighed with pleasure. She could feel an unmistakable tumescence nudging her buttocks. Then his other hand slid down her body to press against her belly, his fingertips cupping her pubis.

His breath was warm on her neck as he bent his head to kiss her there. He nibbled her shoulder and

128

Danni sighed again, pressing herself back harder against him. Squirming her hips, she rubbed her bottom deliberately against his erection.

'Later, Danni,' he groaned, his fingers massaging her breasts and sex, 'I promise you, tonight it will be just us.'

Thrilled at the prospect, Danni turned her head and offered her mouth to his. Their kiss was deep and passionate, kindling a fire deep inside her.

With obvious reluctance, Ivan relaxed his hold around her. 'Come on,' he said gruffly, 'we should start your first lesson.' Untying the rope that tethered the trapeze to the ladder, he held the bar steady so that Danni could climb onto it. 'Just treat it like a children's swing,' he advised her. 'You saw what Guido was doing?'

Danni nodded dumbly. Her whole body was trembling as she sat gingerly on the narrow bar. Reaching out, she held on to the sides of the trapeze with both hands and watched as the blood drained quickly from her knuckles.

'Relax,' Ivan urged, 'this is no worse than a fairground ride.'

'I hate fairs,' Danni muttered. 'The rides scare me to death and so does this.'

Ivan pursed his lips, though his eyes were smiling. 'In that case,' he said, 'I'd better be cruel to be kind.' With that he pushed Danni away from him and before she knew what was happening, she was swinging in mid-air. 'Work your legs and body,' he called to her. 'That's right, backwards and forwards. Go on, keep it up, you're doing it.'

As she huffed and puffed, trying to work up some impetus, she suddenly felt as though she were flying. The relief and sense of freedom it gave her were indescribable. Up there, way above the circus ring, with the white canvas roof just a little way above her head, she felt as though she and the trapeze were one. Swooping back and forth, faster and faster, her body and limbs moved like pistons and she had the overwhelming sensation of being truly free and capable of anything.

She glanced over her shoulder at Ivan's smiling face and returned his smile broadly and confidently. A moment later she risked a glance down. Everything below her swam. She could see people moving about on the ground. The orange mesh of the safety net became a blur. For a moment her arms and legs stopped working and she felt frozen by panic. The trapeze, having lost its motivation, wobbled. Consequently Danni wobbled with it. Her palms, damp with perspiration lost their grip. Then she was falling . . . down and down . . .

Like a bungee, the safety lunge reached its limit then slackened. Her body jerked upwards and as she bounced up and down on the end of the lunge she felt as limp and helpless as a rag doll.

From somewhere above her head she heard Ivan shout, 'Hold on, I'm coming down.'

If she hadn't been so shocked by what was happening, she might have laughed. Hold on – to what? She was suspended in mid-air by a length of elastic. What did he think she was going to do apart from dangle?

Rose and Lettie joined Ivan as he climbed onto the net and reached up to unfasten the safety lunge around Danni's waist.

'Just drop into my arms,' Ivan instructed as Rose unfastened the last buckle.

Danni did as she was told, dropping like a dead weight into Ivan's outstretched arms and causing him to topple backwards into the net. They lay in a tangled heap of arms and legs, Danni crying with relief and also embarrassment at having fallen from the trapeze.

'I mucked it all up,' she wailed, gulping back her sobs.

Ivan's hand was soothing as it stroked her hair. 'Rubbish,' he said firmly. 'Everyone takes a tumble at one time or another.'

Through wet lashes, Danni gazed at him.

'Even you?'

His smile warmed her and he nodded gently. 'Yes,' he said, kissing her forehead. 'Even me.'

It didn't take Danni long to get her equilibrium back and by lunchtime she was quite ready to join the jolly group gathered around the kitchen table. To her surprise she found that she was starving. Temporarily forgetting about her desire to achieve a figure as sylph-like as Fauve's, she tucked into the simple meal of ham, granary bread and salad with gusto.

Lettie and Rose were quick to reassure Danni about her acrobatic abilities, insisting that they had both been terrible on the trapeze at first.

'I won't go up there now unless I have to,' Lettie

confided in her. 'I came to realise quite early on that I was much better suited to other ground-based things.'

'Lettie's a bit of a contortionist,' Ivan supplied as he winked at the young redhead. 'It must give her lovers a thrill.'

You mean you don't already have firsthand experience? Danni wanted to say but she kept her mouth shut and instead smiled at Lettie.

'Well,' Ivan went on, glancing at the clock on the wall, 'I think that's enough conversation, we've got work to do.' He rubbed his hands together and looked meaningfully at Danni, who popped the last piece of her bread into her mouth and stood up.

'Are we going back up on the trapeze this afternoon?' she asked as they walked back out into the sunshine.

Ivan raised his eyebrows as he looked at her. 'On a full stomach?' he said.

Part of Danni was relieved, yet she felt anxious to get back on to the trapeze before she lost her nerve.

'Tomorrow,' he promised her when she told him how she felt.

'This afternoon I plan to show off a bit.'

He told her to go over to the mats and just do some gentle stretching exercises while he sorted out his equipment.

Danni sniggered in a very unladylike way when he said this and wondered immediately afterwards if she would ever get the hang of being sophisti-cated. When he came back he was wheeling a large round board and over his shoulder was slung a green canvas bag. The board was painted red, with a large white star in the centre.

'What's that for?' Danni called out to him as he adjusted the castors on the board frame so that it stood firm on the ground.

'You will see, Danni,' he replied mysteriously. 'Just you concentrate on warming up your muscles. I want you to practise your backflips in a moment.'

Danni immediately regretted the amount she had eaten for lunch. Reaching forward to her toes, with her legs spread wide, she glanced sideways to see what Ivan was doing. She noticed that he had opened the bag and was now taking out a handful of long, broad-bladed knives. It was then she remembered Al telling her that Ivan was famous for his knife-throwing act. Wondering who he used as his assistant – or rather victim – she grasped her left ankle and bent her neck, easing herself down until her forehead touched her knee.

Just as she held the pose, two hands followed the curve of her waist and hips and slid along her thighs. 'Lovely and supple,' Ivan murmured approvingly in her ear.

Her face was hidden by her hair, allowing Danni to smile secretively to herself. She felt instantly warm again, as she always did when Ivan touched her. As she straightened up, she glanced at him over her shoulder.

'Fancy a quick tumble on the mats?' she asked provocatively.

They both glanced around. For once the circus tent was empty of people other than themselves.

Ivan smiled as he slid his hands back up over her sinuous torso and cupped her breasts. 'Don't mind if I do.'

Feeling only slightly concerned that someone might interrupt them, Danni quickly stripped off her leotard. Lying on her side on the mats, her head propped in her hand, she watched Ivan undress. He wore nothing underneath his shorts. And as he pulled them down, she was gratified to see how eagerly his cock sprang free and how hard it was already.

Telling her to stay on her side, Ivan gently pushed her knees up to her chest. Her sex pouted invitingly and it took only the briefest of caresses for Ivan to make her properly wet and eager for him to enter her. As he pushed hard inside her welcoming vagina, Ivan reached up with one hand and stroked her breasts. The nipples sprang to attention and he pinched and pulled at them gently as he ground more deeply into her.

Pulling her knees back towards her chest even more, Danni opened up to him completely, working her hips so that her body and Ivan's ground against each other in perfect harmony. As their tempo increased, Ivan was forced to use both hands flat on the mat to support his weight.

Gazing through her lashes at him, noticing the way his stomach muscles rippled as he moved, Danni felt consumed with lust. She twisted her body at the waist so that her shoulders lay flat against the mats. Sensuously, provocatively, she caressed her own breasts, noticing, when she glanced at Ivan's face, how his gaze darkened as she did so.

He moved then, freeing one hand which he stroked over the curve of her hip. He caressed her buttocks, avidly watching the way his cock slid in and out of her moist opening. The slick wet proof of her arousal rimmed the base of his cock and glistened on the stretched outer lips that surrounded her vagina.

'Beautiful,' he breathed, sliding his hand over her hip and buttocks again, 'exquisite.'

Danni felt the warmth of her arousal flood her and she urged her body against his. Knowing that he was watching his cock move in and out of her made her feel even more aroused. She wished then that they had a mirror, so that she could witness the phenomenon for herself. Just imagining it pushed her over the edge into orgasmic bliss.

Ivan came a few moments later, encouraging Danni to murmur, *'You're* beautiful,' as she watched his face transform into a blissful expression. To her he looked like a god, or a figure from a great work of art. His features were so finely sculpted, his expression so otherworldly that he didn't seem real.

As they came slowly back down to earth and Ivan held her in his arms, her head nestling on his shoulder, she told herself what a lucky girl she was. If Tam hadn't gone off like that . . . if she hadn't happened to read that magazine . . .

'It must be fate,' she murmured quietly to herself. Then she turned her face up and smiled at Ivan. 'Thank you,' she said softly, shaking her head when Ivan asked her what she was thanking him for. 'Just – thank you,' she repeated.

And Ivan, knowing better than to try to fathom the workings of this extraordinary young woman's mind, merely smiled and accepted her words as the compliment they were intended to be.

Their interlude was brief. Being the hard taskmaster that he was, Ivan was soon urging Danni to get back to work. And, after an hour or so of tumbling about on the mats, Danni sprang to her feet and declared that she had had enough. Even though she felt exhausted, her face was flushed with vigour and her eyes sparkling as she smiled triumphantly at Ivan.

'Well done,' he said, smoothing back her hair which tumbled haphazardly around her shoulders. He bunched her hair into a ponytail and held it away from the back of her neck as he kissed it.

Danny felt a small thrill run through her and she stroked her palm across his chest. 'More?' she asked, knowing he would realise that she didn't mean backflips or somersaults.

Dropping her hair, he shook his head regretfully. But he smiled as he said, 'Not just now. I should really put in a little practice. I haven't thrown in over a week.'

He took her hand and led her over to the circular board. Then he positioned her in front of it.

Immediately, Danni stepped away from it. 'Oh, no,' she said. 'Don't think for one minute that I'm going to—'

'Please, Danni,' Ivan interrupted. He put his finger to her lips to quell her protests, then led her back to the place he had put her before.

Shaking her head, Danni protested, 'I can't. I'll move and get my arm chopped off or something. I don't want to die this young.'

Ivan couldn't help laughing. 'I can assure you, sweetheart,' he said, 'you will not die. Nor even lose as much as the tip of a finger.' He moved her arms and legs so that her body formed an X-shape. 'I am the best knife-thrower in the world. You must learn to trust me.'

'I do,' she protested, 'but not with sharp instruments. Not when it's my body at stake.' She glanced at the pile of knives lying on the floor and added pleadingly, 'Look, I know what's going to happen. As soon as you throw one of those things I'll try to move out of the way. It's instinct, isn't it?'

'Instinctive,' Ivan corrected her grammar.

Danni found this amusing considering that she was the one who was English and said so.

'Don't use me, please,' she added, laughing, 'I mean it. I'll only muck it up.'

He looked at her levelly. 'Do you really think you would move?'

'I'd run a bloody mile,' Danni answered with feeling.

'Then there's only one thing for it,' Ivan responded, advancing towards her.

137

Glancing around, Danni felt a surge of expectation. What was he planning to do? To her surprise he grabbed one of her wrists and secured it to the board with a leather cuff. Then he did the same with her other wrist.

'No!' Danni shouted, trying to squirm. 'This is a joke, isn't it, Ivan?'

'No joke,' he said, strapping her ankles in a similar fashion, ignoring the way she tried to ward him off by kicking out at him.

Strapped in a spread-eagle position on the round board, Danni glared furiously at him. It annoyed her the way Ivan treated the whole thing as a game and yet at the same time she couldn't help feeling deliciously helpless. He could do anything to her while she was like this, she realised with a thrill of nervous anticipation, and she wouldn't be able to do a damn thing to stop him.

'You are just planning to throw knives at me, aren't you?' she said, thinking, '*just* knives!' and almost laughing at the ridiculousness of her predicament.

'No,' he replied with a shake of his head. He reached into the green holdall and took out a set of wicked-looking implements that Danni recognised from watching old westerns on TV. 'I thought I'd practise with the tomahawks as well.'

Then she did laugh. She continued laughing until tears of disbelief at what she'd got herself into ran down her face and Ivan told her to stop because her shoulders were shaking.

'You must remain perfectly still,' he warned,

coming over to her and placing his hands on her shoulders and stroking them until she calmed down. 'Please, Danni. No harm is going to come to you and playing the hysterical female doesn't suit you one bit.'

Danni hung her head in shame. Hysteria had almost got the better of her and now Ivan was treating her like a frightened animal. His touch was soothing and soon she felt herself relax and simply give in to the pleasure of his caresses. When she stopped shaking, his hands slid across her collarbone and then down over the wall of her chest to her breasts.

She sighed as he moulded them gently and whispered soothing words in her ear.

'I'm not going to hurt you, Danni sweetheart,' he said. 'Please believe me, I have spent many years practising this art. I am the best.'

There was nothing modest about his claim and yet he made it without a hint of conceit.

'I'm sorry, Ivan,' Danni said finally as she raised her head to look him in the eye.

He smiled a crinkly, sparkling-eyed smile that melted her heart and the rest of her insides.

'Don't be,' he admonished her gently, 'I've said it before and I'll say it again – just trust me.'

'I do,' she said earnestly, knowing deep down that she meant it, 'it's me I don't trust.' She paused then added, 'It's a bit like – oh, I don't know – a bit like when you're standing on a station platform and you know the train's coming and all of a sudden you get this wild urge to jump onto the track.'

'You do?' He sounded amused.

'Well, *I* do,' Danni asserted, 'I suppose that makes me sound a bit mad.'

Ivan's hands left her breasts to stroke her hair and follow the contours of her face. He cupped her face in his hands and looked levelly at her.

'I suppose it does,' he said with a straight face, 'after all, anyone who is prepared to stand there and let me throw knives at them must be completely crazy.'

'Careful,' she said, laughing all over again, 'otherwise when I get free of this thing I'll throw a few knives at you.'

As it turned out, Ivan proved himself beyond a shadow of doubt in Danni's mind that he was extremely skilful. He threw the knives and tomahawks apparently casually but with accurate precision so that they dug into the wood just fractions of an inch from her body.

After he had got into his stride and when Danni assured him that she now trusted his skill completely, Ivan went on to the next stage of his act which involved rotating the wheel.

As Danni spun round and round she felt herself becoming dizzy. So much so that the sound of the blades whizzing towards her and digging into the wooden board hardly compared with the tide of blood rushing in her ears. It was as though someone had stuck a couple of seashells to the sides of her head. In the end she gave up trying to fight the sensation and instead closed her eyes. She kept them tightly shut until Ivan was satisfied that he had had enough practice for one day.

As he slowed the spinning board and brought it to a halt with his hand, he said, 'You can open them now, it's all over.'

'Thank God,' Danni responded with a huge sigh of relief. 'Now you can get me out of these things.' She pulled ineffectually against the wrist restraints.

Just as Ivan reached up to unbuckle the first one, they were interrupted by the arrival of Lettie and Rose. The two young women were both dressed in jeans and cropped white T-shirts that showed off their narrow midriffs.

'Phone call for you, Ivan,' Lettie said.

He glanced over his shoulder at her and stepped back. 'Oh, really? I had better go and see who it is.'

'What about me?' Danni said, trying not to sound plaintive.

Lettie grinned at her and then at Ivan. 'Don't worry,' she said to Ivan, 'Rose and I will sort Danni out for you. You'd better not hang about, I think the call is long distance.'

As soon as Ivan had gone Lettie turned to Danni again. 'You're brave,' she murmured approvingly. Then she nodded in Rose's direction. 'Isn't she brave, sis?'

Rose said she was and then to Danni's complete surprise, walked up to her and ran a hand assessingly over her torso. 'Do you know what, Lettie?' she said, reaching for something in the back pocket of her jeans, 'I think it's a bit too soon to undo those restraints. Danni deserves some fun and relaxation after allowing herself to be put through such a dreadful ordeal.'

'Oh, no, it wasn't that bad—' Danni started to protest but her words evaporated into thin air as she caught sight of the long, white, ribbed plastic vibrator Rose was now holding.

Lettie grinned at her sister, then at Danni. She took the vibrator from Rose and turned the base. As the vibrator whirred into life Danni sensed their purpose and felt her stomach turn inside out. This was no premonition. There was no mistaking exactly how the twins planned to help her to relax. And she was totally powerless to stop them.

Chapter Eight

THE SWEET WOODCHIP smell of sawdust mingled with patchouli oil would always remind Danni of that afternoon in the circus tent. Both twins favoured the scent of patchouli. They told Danni that they wore it as a sort of homage to their mother, who had been an original sixties flower child. Free love, they said as they caressed Danni's body over the top of her leotard, was an expression of everything beautiful.

If Danni hadn't felt so helpless, or so full of anxiety about being left at the tender mercy of the two young women, she might have laughed at this.

As it was she said, 'I really don't think this sort of thing is for me.'

Rose glanced up at her wide-eyed. She was kneeling in front of Danni, her pale fine-boned hands exploring the contours of her legs.

'How do you know until you've tried it?' she asked simply. 'You enjoyed last night, didn't you?'

Danni sighed and tried to organise her thoughts

and feelings so that she could express them as succinctly as possible without sounding hurtful.

'Yes, I did enjoy it,' she said finally, 'but that was different. I'd had a lot to drink and Al—'

'You liked it regardless, why deny it?' Lettie cut in, running the tip of the vibrator back and forth across Danni's throat and the upper swell of her breasts.

'I'm not denying it,' Danni insisted, trying to twist her body away from the vibrator and finding herself hopelessly pinned down, 'I'm just explaining why it was different then compared to now.'

'But now it's just us,' Rose said soothingly. 'No audience. No men.' She stood up and took the vibrator away from her sister. Over the top of Danni's leotard, she circled each of her breasts with the throbbing instrument. The circles became smaller and smaller until they were concentrated around Danni's nipples. 'There's no need to feel embarrassed,' she added, still in a gentle tone.

To Danni's shame, she felt her body respond to the tingling vibrations. It wasn't the first time she had experienced the inanimate pleasure that a vibrator could give her. But before, she had always been the one in charge of the device. Herself alone, locked in her own private world of self-induced gratification.

Now, it seemed, as far as her treacherous body was concerned, the inclusion of other people didn't make the slightest difference to its responses. She could feel her torso start to hum, echoing the erotic tune the vibrator plucked from

144

her sensitive nerve endings. Her nipples stiffened and, further down, her sex began to tingle as her vagina moistened.

Don't do this to me, body, she moaned silently. A gasp of surprise escaped her as Lettie's fingers slid under the scrap of fabric covering her pubic mound. The fingers stroked her pubis and gently pulled the skin upwards, parting her outer labia. Then Lettie slid her hand all the way between Danni's legs, her knowing fingers spreading the labia wider apart and skimming tantalisingly around the sensitive flesh rimming Danni's vagina.

Danni tried hard to stifle a whimper. She could feel her body answering Lettie's caresses with a continuous pulse of excitement. And she could sense the way her outer labia swelled and opened out like petals to reveal the dewy, sensitive flesh beneath.

What a shame she's wearing this thing,' Lettie said with a glance at her sister.

Rose nodded. 'I know, it's a nuisance, isn't it?' she agreed, 'mind you, if it were to tear—' She broke off to pull experimentally at the neckline of the leotard.

To Danni's relief, although she thought she felt it give slightly, the fabric stayed in one piece. Her relief was short-lived. In the next moment Lettie picked up one of Ivan's knives. A shaft of sunlight caught the blade sending a flash of light across her face as she held it up.

'We could cut it with this,' she said to Rose, 'it'll

be all the easier to repair afterwards, otherwise we'll have Fauve on our backs.'

Rose's eyes sparkled wickedly as she nodded and suggested she hold the material taut while her sister cut it. The knife was sinfully sharp and sliced through the thin fabric as easily as if it were melted butter. Within seconds the front of the leotard was slashed from neck to navel.

'Now for the crotch,' Lettie said, 'hold it fast for me would you, Rose?'

'Now just a minute—' Danni protested. It frustrated her that they were treating her like a plaything, as though she had no say in the matter.

Rose glanced up at Danni as she squatted down and pulled the damp fabric away from her crotch. She held it taut between her fingers.

'Just trust us, Danni,' she said, sounding uncannily like Ivan, 'soon you'll be screaming with lust.'

'I won't,' Danni said defiantly, hoping she could resist the torment of the vibrator and prove them wrong.

She recoiled as she felt both Lettie and Rose's fingers brushing her sex and then winced as her warm flesh received a cold glance of steel.

'Mind you don't cut her,' Rose warned her sister, 'that wouldn't be much fun.'

The twins laughed and Danni fumed at their amusement at her expense. This was all so embarrassing and unfair. Where the hell was Ivan, why hadn't he come back yet? All at once, a disconcerting thought struck her. Just supposing the whole thing was planned. But no, surely not? Ivan wouldn't dream of doing that to her – would he? Although she was dying to ask the twins to tell her the truth, she didn't dare because deep down she didn't want to know the answer. She preferred to believe that Ivan would return at any moment and be shocked at the way the twins were taking advantage of her.

'There,' Lettie said with satisfaction a moment later, 'one totally free pussy.'

Danni hated that particular description and wanted to say so. She glanced down and noticed how the leotard now hung between her legs. The front flap protected her modesty visually although she could feel the caress of fresh air on her exposed groin. It was unarguably tantalising and she felt all the more embarrassed by her predicament. Her mind was saying one thing while her body was saying something else. Feeling the moisture drying around her vagina as another warm breath of air whipped between her legs she looked anxiously towards the big top entrance, willing Ivan to appear.

'Don't you think this has gone far enough now,' she protested feebly, 'after all, a joke's a joke but—'

From their squatting position in front of her, Lettie and Rose both glanced up at her and then at each other.

'Did you hear that, sis?' Rose said, 'She thinks we're playing a bit of a prank.' Both sisters looked up at Danni again, their expressions completely sincere.

'We both enjoy other women's bodies, Danni,'

Lettie explained, encouraged by nods from Rose, 'and men's. We're not lesbians, we're bisexual and proud of it.' She paused and laughed. 'Apart from anything else, it gives us twice the amount of scope for pleasure. We were hoping you would enjoy our attentions. You will,' she added, more vehemently this time, 'I promise you, you will love what we're going to do to you.'

By this time Danni felt as though she had no option but to give in gracefully. There was no way she could fight them, nor even dissuade them. And in the back of her mind a small voice kept telling her to simply go with the flow. You might enjoy it, the voice said, why deny yourself the promise of pleasure just because the situation is different from what you are used to?

She felt her breath catch and held it as Lettie said to Rose, 'Let's tuck this bit out of the way.'

Warm air caressed her belly as the scrap of fabric hanging down at the front was raised and tucked under what was left of the leotard. She felt incredibly exposed now that she was completely naked from the waist down, with her legs spread and shackled wide apart.

'Pretty little pussy,' Lettie crooned, kneeling on the floor and stroking her hand over Danni's mound. 'Isn't she lovely, Rose?'

The other twin murmured that Danni's sex was indeed lovely and also knelt on the ground to peer between her legs.

Danni felt a flush of shame which started at the tips of her toes and spread throughout her body.

The way the two girls were looking at her most intimate parts and describing what they saw was lewd and yet intolerably exciting. Most of her shame was the result of her own arousal. It didn't seem right to get so turned on by the situation. But aroused she was. She could feel her clitoris swelling and pushing its way between her blossoming outer lips. And her juices were running so freely that they were trickling down the insides of her thighs.

Rose started the vibrator again and stroked it along Danni's sex. A moan escaped Danni's lips. The humming of the instrument sent tingles through her entire body. Her clitoris swelled a little more each time the tip of the vibrator glanced over and around it.

'Nice, huh?' Rose said to her with a smile.

Danni managed to nod. Her whole body felt warm and liquid. If she hadn't been strapped to the board she fancied she might easily have melted into the sawdust. Rose was clever with the vibrator. Somehow, Danni realised, she managed to orchestrate her body to the point of climax and then transfer the pleasure to another part of her anatomy, so that she was left hanging – literally and metaphorically.

The need to orgasm became paramount. Danni heard herself moaning and whimpering, pleading with the girls to let her come.

'Ah, no, not yet,' Lettie teased as she watched her sister draw the tip of the vibrator along the taut length of Danni's inner thigh. 'We want to see how far we can take your pleasure. I promise you, when you do come, it will be explosive.'

Danni didn't doubt it. The vibrator was circling her clitoris again and she felt like exploding now. In her feverish state of mind it seemed to her that her entire body consisted only of her vulva. It dominated every scrap of her senses. She could see it in her mind's eye, all red and swollen and juicy. She could feel the way it throbbed and tingled and moistened. And while her ears were filled with the soft whirring of the vibrator, her nostrils were suffused with the scent of her own arousal.

While Rose stayed kneeling between Danni's outstretched legs and continued to stroke and tease her urgent flesh, Lettie straightened up and stood by Danni's side. Gently, she reached out and parted the front of the leotard so that Danni's breasts were bared. The tanned globes sat high and rounded on her ribcage, the nipples swollen and deeply roseate.

'Lovely breasts,' Lettie breathed admiringly as she simply gazed at them.

Rose glanced up. 'Aren't they?' she concurred, 'Don't they make you feel envious, sis?'

'Mm, absolutely but at least I get to play with them.'

Lettie smoothed her hands up Danni's ribcage and cupped the breasts from underneath, her thumb and forefinger capturing the nipples. She pulled and pinched at them slightly and gave a sigh of satisfaction as they hardened. Smiling straight into Danni's face, which was bright red with a mixture of arousal and mortification, she added, 'You're a very lucky girl to have such a lovely body, Danni. I don't know why you're so shy about revelling in it and showing it off.'

Danni couldn't speak. She tried to but she couldn't. At that point all she could do was signal with her eyes that she was enjoying the twins' caresses. Her lids felt heavy, weighted with lust. It seemed no part of her body went unexplored by the two sisters. While Lettie caressed her breasts, arms and torso, Rose's hands took it in turns to lightly travelled the length of her legs, while she played the vibrator over different parts of her lower body. Softly stroking fingers and the tip of the humming instrument excited the sensitive flesh of Danni's inner thighs, at the backs of her knees, circled her ankles and even stroked between her toes.

A glorious sense of her own womanliness suffused Danni. She felt capable of so much. Her skin and the muscles beneath – stretched taut by necessity of her spread-eagled position – were receptive to every caress. Sensations of voluptuous warmth coursed through every part of her. Her body was an instrument which the twins, through their natural curiosity and sensuality, were able to fine tune and ultimately create harmonious melodies of eroticism.

When she was finally allowed to come, Danni's orgasm was so volatile that she cried out loudly. Her body trembled convulsively until the board – which had been staunch under siege by knives and tomahawks – began to rock. Lettie grasped at it and held it fast without removing her mouth from Danni's breast. Rose, with her fingers buried deep inside Danni, glanced up at her sister.

'Like a volcano erupting,' she said with a hint of amusement. 'I knew she would be like this.'

Returning to reality on the ebbing flow of her orgasm, Danni blushed and smiled weakly.

'I'm sorry,' she said as soon as she had got her breath back, 'I didn't mean to get carried away.'

Rose laughed then and, as she sat back on her heels, her fingers slid out of the moist channel of Danni's vagina. Raising them to her mouth, Rose licked each finger with deliberate relish and a suggestive twinkle in her eye. Turning off the vibrator she stroked the pulsating folds of Danni's vulva tenderly.

'No need to apologise,' she said. 'You obviously loved it.'

'Yes,' Danni said simply.

It shamed her to have to concede defeat after the strength of her denials. Yet at the same time she felt as though another tiny piece of her had been liberated.

Lettie allowed her mouth and hands to slide from Danni's breasts. She left a wet trail down her torso as she sank to the floor. Her lips and tongue pressed to Danni's body for as long as they were able. Then she sat cross-legged and serene beside her sister who copied Lettie's pose.

The warm caress of the late afternoon breeze dried Danni's skin instantly and she felt a small pang of remorse that the encounter, which had seemed so daunting at the start, had now come to an end. To Danni's delight, Lettie's fingers joined those of her sister in a twin caress of her feminine flesh. Lettie stroked her clitoris lightly, smiling knowingly when the tiny bud, so sensitive now, seemed to recoil from her fingers and the muscles in Danni's thighs and groin tensed.

'Can't take any more, huh?' she asked gently.

All three of them jumped when a smoothly accented voice suddenly came out of nowhere and demanded, 'What is this? A case of while the cat is away, I think.'

Ivan! Danni breathed a sigh of relief that he had returned. Then she felt immediately guilty, wondering what he would make of their situation.

'I couldn't stop them,' Danni said as she sensed him walk up behind her.

She felt guilty again then, as though her declaration of helpless innocence betrayed the twins' good intentions. Still, she reasoned, so what if she had enjoyed it? She *had* been helpless. Neither of the twins had given her a choice. What if their actions had turned out to have the opposite effect, leaving her sexuality scarred for life?

The curve of Ivan's lips and the twinkle in his deep blue eyes told Danni that he saw through her charade.

'Danni, Danni,' he murmured, stroking her bare breasts, 'there is nothing to be ashamed of here. Except perhaps—' he paused and glanced down at the twins, who still sat on the sawdust covered floor, their expressions now a little sheepish, 'these two should know better than to take such blatant advantage of someone.'

Displaying characteristic inconsistency, Danni was quick to defend them. 'Oh, I'm sure they didn't mean any harm. And I did – I did—' '

'Did what, Danni?' Ivan raised an imperious eyebrow, although the smile in his eyes softened his expression.

'Did enjoy it in the end,' she mumbled, wondering whether to blush or laugh. In the end she did both.

'Come on, you,' Ivan said after a moment. He reached for the strap tethering her right ankle. 'I think it is time I released you.' For a second or two he hesitated and glanced at Rose and Lettie who stood up, grumbling. 'Or perhaps—' he teased. His tone of voice and the insolent expression on his face dared Danni to argue, or plead. When she did neither and simply pretended to ignore him, he laughed again. 'Just joking,' he said, then he added, 'A few of us are going down to the lake for a swim, would you girls like to come along?'

Lettie and Rose agreed eagerly, their faces all smiles. Ivan glanced at Danni as he moved to unfasten the restraints around her wrists.

'Yes, please,' she said, feeling doubly relieved at the prospect of being released and of enjoying a simple pleasure for a change. Going for a dip in a lake seemed like the perfect end to a very odd, but not unpleasant, afternoon.

*

Sunlight glinted off the water of the small, elliptical lake which was surrounded by a grassy meadow. Beyond its boundary was a thickly wooded area of oak, elm, sycamore and silver birch. The lush emerald grass of the meadow was strewn with dasies and clumps of clover. And Danni discovered if she screwed her eyes up slightly, the meadow looked for all the world like an unrolled bolt of green and white patterned fabric.

The surroundings were tranquil and Danni thought the lake idyllic in the way it shimmered like a gemstone in the centre of the meadow. The colour of the glassy water was a brilliant turquoise. Its iridescence was so inviting that Danni couldn't wait to wade into the lake's cool depths and swim until she was completely exhausted. She hadn't brought a bathing suit or bikini with her. But that hardly seemed to matter as no one else in their small group – which consisted of herself, Ivan, the twins, Randi and Guido – seemed all that bothered about costumes.

'Skinny-dipping, my second favourite thing in the whole world,' Lettie claimed dramatically as she dragged off her T-shirt and jeans. Underneath, her slim pale body was completely naked.

The twins' white bodies, tinted only by a scattering of freckles, seemed a sharp contrast to those of everyone else. Although her skin wasn't naturally olive-toned like that of Ivan or Guido, Danni felt her own golden brown hue was equally attractive. And having a tan always made her feel thinner and more athletic somehow. As she shrugged off the yellow cotton dress she had put on to replace the ruined leotard and scampered quickly down to the water's edge, she felt sublimely free. Perhaps not free enough to parade around with the utmost confidence, like Lettie and Rose, but certainly more relaxed about being naked in mixed company.

Although weakening a little, the rays from the sun were still warm on her back. She felt them toasting her buttocks and shoulders as she stepped gingerly into the water. Recoiling a little from the coolness of the lake, she felt her toes sinking into the mud at the bottom. The water was clear enough for her to see where she was treading. Only a few large pebbles were scattered about on the lake bed and she was able to walk quite confidently into the water until it was waist high. Then she took a deep breath, preparing to submerge the rest of her body in its cool depths.

Fighting the initial shock, which made her want to run back to the water's edge and shiver under a towel, she struck out for the far side of the lake. It was wider than it looked and by the time she was able to touch the bottom again her chest was heaving with the effort of her swim. When she looked up she saw a familiar pair of lean brown legs.

'You look like a particularly beautiful water nymph,' Ivan said. As he squatted down by the edge of the lake, he offered her a helping hand.

Her feet squelched in the mud – a sensation that Danni was surprised to find quite sensuous. All at once, a devilish idea occurred to her. It would serve him right, she thought, and in the next moment she yanked hard on Ivan's arm. Just as she expected, he toppled forward, falling headlong into the lake.

Water droplets sprayed from the ends of his hair as he surfaced, shaking his head like a shaggy dog and gasping for breath.

Danni started laughing. She couldn't help herself and Ivan pretended to look annoyed.

'Cheeky little minx,' he growled with mock ferocity. 'I'll have to make you pay for that.'

Taking her by surprise he grabbed her round the waist and the two of them play-tussled until they fell, gasping and shaking with laughter, onto the muddy bank. Ivan began to tickle Danni and, as she tried to squirm out of his grasp, she became coated with the sticky ooze.

'Mm,' she murmured, squelching her hands into the mud and smearing handfuls over her breasts. After a moment lost in total abandon, she realised Ivan was watching her and not saying anything. 'What?' she said, looking up at him wide-eyed. She noticed he was wearing the sort of wolfish expression that she had seen a few times before – usually as a prelude to lovemaking. 'Are you thinking what I'm thinking?' she asked with only a hint of surprise.

Ivan pretended to look confused. 'How could I know what you are thinking?' he asked. 'The working of your mind is a mystery to me.'

'What about the working of my body?' Danni

countered, mimicking the way he spoke. She couldn't help noticing how hard her nipples had become and felt her body dissolve into the soft mud.

'Ah, that,' he murmured throatily while stroking a questioning hand over her mud-spattered torso. 'Your body is a different matter entirely.'

As his fingers delved between her legs, Danni whimpered with pleasure. Her arousal was instantaneous. Although she sank further into the mud she spread her legs wide apart, her hands coming up to stroke Ivan's chest and shoulders. She smiled at the handprints she left on him and then gasped as she felt his fingers sink inside her.

Her immediate reaction was to try and stop him. 'Don't,' she hissed urgently, 'someone might see.'

'Let them,' Ivan said, fingering her more deeply, 'let them see me caressing you. They will only feel envious.'

She warmed to his compliment and the strength of passion he invoked in her. The others could not be seen from where she lay and Danni soon gave up all pretence at modesty. Churning her sex against his hand she reached down and grasped the hard rod of his penis. For once she didn't fancy putting it in her mouth, not while it was coated with mud. But later she would, she promised herself. Later she would give him as much pleasure as he was giving her.

He took her almost straight away, in a quick hard manner that left them both breathless and temporarily satisfied. Afterwards they rolled around in the mud like playful seals. Danni and Ivan's hair was plastered with mud and long tendrils, thickened with the gooey mass, clung to their faces and necks.

'We must look a sight,' Danni said, wiping a tendril of hair away from the corner of her mouth and streaking her face in the process.

'You look beautiful,' Ivan assured her.

Smiling down at him as she lay on her side, resting her head in her hand, Danni stroked a single muddy fingertip down the length of his torso.

'So do you,' she said.

Resting on the bank of the lake, the waning sun still warm enough to bake the mud onto their naked bodies, Danni and Ivan talked a little about their pasts and about *Cirque Erotique*.

'I can't believe how much less inhibited I feel,' Danni confessed to him, 'coming here has certainly been an eye opener.'

Stroking her breasts absently, Ivan smiled up at her. 'I always like to think of our bodies as erotic treasure chests,' he said sagely, 'with all our desires and needs locked up inside. All it takes is someone with the right key . . .' He allowed his words to taper off and instead brought Danni's mouth down to meet his for a long, lingering kiss.

'You certainly seem to have been my keyholder,' Danni said when they finally broke apart. She looked at him, feeling the poignancy of passion and realising that she wanted him again.

Moving as gracefully as she could, she straddled his body. Her muddy thighs gripped his hips as her hand sought the reassuring hardness of his cock. Her body was undeniably wet and ready for him and, as she positioned herself over his cock and teasingly circled the rim of her vagina with his glans, she found it so easy to slide right down the length of him, engulfing his penis completely.

She ground her hips, watching his changing expression the whole time. There was no doubt he enjoyed being inside her, making love to her, fucking her, whatever ... And she felt free enough to admit that she enjoyed him. She appreciated his responsiveness and his obvious enthusiasm for her body.

Right now he was reaching for her breasts as they dangled tantalisingly over his chest. A smile of satisfaction crossed his lips and he closed his eyes as he grasped them, his fingers moulding the pliant flesh while she rode him.

With her knees slithering in the soft mud, Danni was forced to grip Ivan really tightly with her thighs. She could feel her excitement mounting by degrees. The hard length of Ivan's cock stroked her inner walls tantalisingly, while she felt the flesh of her labia being stimulated as it rubbed against his pubic bone. Wiping her muddy fingers on a nearby clump of grass, she slid her hand between her legs, stroking her throbbing clitoris until she came in tumultuous waves of sheer pleasure.

With his eyes closed, Ivan was able to concentrate on the delicious movements of Danni's body. His senses delighted to the texture of her vagina, so soft and pulpy, like ripe fruit, yet with an unyielding grip. And the sensation of the soft mud beneath him, the fresh floral scent of the meadow and the delicate warmth of the waning sun combined to embrace him with a voluptuous sensuality.

As his hands cupped and moulded Danni's breasts he felt the soft scratching of her fingernails on his lower belly. A smile touched his lips. She was pleasuring herself. Opening his eyes only a fraction, he watched her covertly, enjoying the obvious proof of her enjoyment. She looked radiant, her cheeks flushed, her gaze sultry and heavy-lidded with lust. He felt her tremble. Sensing the sudden tightening of her body, he knew that she was approaching climax. His hands left her breasts to grip her hips and he slammed upwards into her. He kept up a rhythm of short, fast thrusts until he heard her anguished whimpers and felt the tell-tale spasming of her vaginal muscles.

Still riding him hard, she milked him. The harmonious grip and relaxation of her inner muscles drained him of every last drop of passion. And when they were finally spent he felt the delightful weight and warmth of her naked body as she collapsed on top of him. For a few moments they basked in the aftermath of plea-sure, their bodies still joined. With eyes closed they shared the final abating tremors of their mutual orgasm and the rhythm of each other's heartbeat. The only sounds to break the stillness were the cries of the birds that darted across the blank blue canvas of the sky above them, and the steadying rhythm of their own breathing.

For both of them it was an experience to savour. A perfect moment captured within the landscape of time.

Chapter Nine

BY SATURDAY AFTERNOON, Danni was no longer afraid to swing on the trapeze and had also learned to juggle. She was proud of both achievements but throwing three clubs in the air and catching them ten times in a row struck her as one of the most triumphant moments of her life.

Al was an expert juggler and he showed her how to hold two clubs in her dominant hand, throw one of them and wait until it turned in the air before throwing the single club in her subordinate hand. Time and again she dropped the second club, instead of throwing it, in her eagerness to catch the first. It was frustrating but Al proved very patient. Each time he simply told her to pick up the dropped club and start again.

Taking the clubs from her, he showed her how to throw the clubs high to give herself extra time.

'Every time the club spins, throw the next one,' he said, 'and remember to alternate your hands and concentrate on smooth scoops.'

When she found her skill with three clubs

getting worse instead of improving, he made her go back to using just two clubs and then one, until she regained her confidence again.

'I'm hopeless at this,' she wailed at one point as she scrabbled around in the sawdust picking up not just one dropped club but all three. 'I'll never get the hang of it and it always looks so easy when other people do it.'

'You're not hopeless and you will get it, sweet-pea,' he insisted gently, 'but these things take hours and hours of practice. You can't expect to be brilliant straight away.'

'Oh, but I do,' Danni said grimly as she prepared to throw the first club for the umpteenth time, 'I won't settle for being second best.'

To her annoyance Al laughed. It was a deep rumbling laugh that seemed to echo around the canvas walls of the big top.

'Ain't no worries on that score, honey,' he said, grabbing her around the waist with one hugely muscled arm and squeezing her tight. 'You'll never be second best at anything.'

After that she seemed to do much better. Whether it was Al's compliment, or his confidence in her, she didn't know. What she did know was that if she simply relaxed and concentrated on what she was doing, she could get it right.

Just before lunchtime, Al told her to sit on the ringside and watch him while he showed off a little. He said it in a confident, though not arrogant way that made Danni warm to him even more than she already had.

'Guido's a good juggler,' he said as he played casually with half a dozen brightly coloured hoops. Throwing them into the air, he caught them swiftly, one after the other. Then he juggled them for a few more minutes before adding, 'I'd go as far as to say, Guido is proving to be quite a find.'

'Really?' Danni felt compelled to ask, 'Why is that?'

'Aha,' Al said mysteriously, 'you'll have to wait until tonight. A little birdie told me Fauve and Guido have something special planned.'

Danni nodded sagely and didn't bother to press him. After the experience with Meah, she realised that dinner time often included special treats that would never appear on the menus of most ordinary folk.

After her session with Al, Danni returned to her room and changed into a pair of shorts. She teamed them with a skimpy vest top and went outside again to catch the last of the day's rays. The garden lounger was soft and squashy and covered with blue and white ticking. It wasn't long before weariness and the warmth of the sun overcame her and she fell into a light doze.

She awoke to see Fauve and Ivan strolling across the small patch of paddock which had been edged with shrubs and brightly hued bedding plants to form a garden. Ivan's white-blond head was bent to catch what Fauve was saying to him and every so often he smiled and nodded in agreement. When they reached the small wooden bench which stood in the shade of a spiky-limbed monkey puzzle tree, he and Fauve sat down to continue their conversation.

For once, Danni found herself more interested in observing Fauve than Ivan. She hadn't seen all that much of the older woman during the past few days. When she had mentioned it to Ivan he told her Fauve had a lot of business matters to attend to.

'She is a marvellous woman,' he had said admiringly, 'beautiful and intelligent, a truly unbeatable combination.' The comment had incited a small flicker of jealousy in Danni for which she had reproached herself immediately. If it hadn't been for Fauve's generosity she wouldn't be there at all, and would never have met Ivan.

Today Fauve was wearing an ankle-skimming dress of pleated orange fabric. The colour set off her mahogany tan beautifully and her hair had been slicked back with gel. Like a glossy cap it clung to the delicate structure of her skull and made her look younger and more vulnerable, somehow.

Obviously Ivan liked her hair styled in that way, Danni thought to herself, because he kept reaching out to stroke it, or run the back of a crooked finger over her high curving cheekbone. This particular gesture was achingly familiar to Danni and she was forced to close her eyes eventually, deliberately blocking out the vision before envy overcame her completely.

She knew she had no right to feel resentful of

Ivan's relationship with Fauve. They had known each other forever. she reminded herself, Fauve was probably like a sister to him. All the same, she couldn't help feeling a stab of jealousy every time Ivan spoke about the older woman, because he always referred to her in such glowing terms. Obviously, she thought, in Ivan's eyes at any rate, Fauve could do no wrong. She was the brilliant businesswoman, the graceful hostess, the highly skilled artiste. Whereas Danni was – well – just Danni.

Like the sun coming out on a dull day, the realisation struck her that the only way she could keep up Ivan's interest in her was to become more interesting herself. Straight, sexually unadventurous Danni would not do. Ivan had clearly enjoyed the details she had related to him about her encounter with Lettie and Rose. And he had obviously found their later session on the muddy bank of the lake a rewardingly erotic interlude. Afterwards, he had told her that it would go down in his mental catalogue of hedonistic pleasures as one of the most erotic experiences he had ever had. 'I never realised mud could be so sensual,' he confided in her, 'you taught *me* something there.' As a consequence she had glowed with pleasure for the rest of the evening and hadn't minded when he said he couldn't join her in her room that night because he had some important phone calls to make.

'Business,' he had said disparagingly, 'is an irritating curb to enjoyment but also a necessary evil.'

Danni had accepted his explanation without

trying to persuade him otherwise. But the single night of enforced celibacy had left her feeling extremely amorous. She couldn't wait to get him alone later. And, as she lay on the garden lounger soaking up the last of the sun, she noticed how sexy she felt most of the time now.

It wasn't a word she usually used to describe her feelings, yet it seemed the most appropriate right at that moment. She wasn't sure if she could honestly class herself as truly sensual, feeling that there was so much more to pleasure that she didn't know, or hadn't experienced. So *sexy* would have to do. If there was one thing she was sure about, it was that she was far more aware of her body these days.

Before she came to the circus school she had always enjoyed sexual pleasure, whether in the company of someone else or self-induced. But now it seemed her body had taken on a new dimension. It was as though its needs were far more apparent, and urgent, than they had been before. Just lately, she felt as though her body ruled her mind more often than not, rather than the other way around. She was also far more aware of the different permutations for erotic gratification. One-to-one, man-woman, had always seemed the only way to her to achieve sexual fulfilment.

Just lately her rigid notions had taken a bit of a battering. Now she knew it was possible to enjoy licentious pleasures bestowed by a person of the same sex. Her experience with Lettie and Rose had taught her that much. Whether she could actually derive enjoyment from touching another woman was a dilemma she still hadn't managed to resolve. And she wasn't all that sure whether she wanted to find out.

Just at that moment the memory of Meah's chocolate-button nipples sprang into her mind and she licked her lips in an unconscious gesture. Shifting on the garden lounger to make herself more comfortable, Danni realised that her body had started to respond to the image of its own accord. She felt desirous again. Her juices were flowing, her clitoris wakening and starting its gentle pulse.

Stop it! she told herself firmly, you are not a lesbian, Danni, or even bisexual like the twins. Nevertheless, she was forced to admit that, with each passing day, she was beginning to doubt her long-held belief that she was a man's woman through and through.

At dinner that evening she put on the white dress again. Freshly laundered it stood out well against her golden tan. And, though she wasn't sure if it was just wishful thinking, she fancied she looked more svelte in it. Her hips didn't look quite so – well – hippy, she decided as she appraised herself in the mirror, and her stomach looked almost flat.

Feeling daring, she left off her underwear. Just knowing that she was wearing nothing at all under the dress gave her a thrill of excitement. She might let Ivan in on her naughty secret, or then again she might not. Just to sit there at the table, eating and making conversation, with her sex naked under the short dress would be titillation in itself.

Arriving late, she found everyone already gathered around the table. Everyone that was except Guido. Glancing at Meah, Danni couldn't help thinking how lovely the young woman looked in the shiny emerald green dress she was wearing. Although it was far too dressy for a simple meal with friends – which was how she looked upon Ivan, Fauve and the others – Danni thought the dress was an absolutely perfect adornment for a woman who was already beautiful. Plain and simple, with shoestring straps and a hem that ended mid-thigh, it looked like a sparkling jewel with Meah herself as its exquisite setting.

'Where's Guido?' Danni asked Fauve as she took the only empty seat, which was between the older woman and Al.

The chips of black marble that were Fauve's eyes glittered in the light from three long white candles, which stood in the middle of the table and were set in an hexagonal holder of smoked glass.

She smiled warmly at Danni as she said, 'Guido will be here in a little while, *chérie*. He has chosen to be our waiter for tonight.'

Aha, so that's the plan, Danni thought to herself. Obviously the evening was set to involve an element of après-dinner entertainment.

'You look great tonight, sweetpea,' Al cut in, his smile as warm as Fauve's. His eyes were acutely appraising as they flicked over Danni's body.

She felt herself becoming aroused under the

steady gaze that followed his appraisal. Her nipples hardened and she clenched her thighs tightly together to quell the tingling that had started up between them.

'You too,' she managed to gasp.

It was the truth. Normally fabulous-looking anyway, Al was looking particularly delectable in white jeans that clung to his enviably rounded bottom and strong, muscular thighs. With these he wore a lime-green piqué shirt which looked startlingly good in contrast with his tanned skin. Sinewy biceps bulged under the short sleeves and the rest of the fabric fitted like a second skin to his broad torso, showing off every curve of his musculature.

Varying hues of green seemed to be the fashion statement of the evening, Danni noticed as she glanced around the table at the others. Apart from Meah and Al, Ivan was also in green – an olive-green silk shirt, teamed with linen trousers – and Rose was wearing a pair of green and white striped baggy cotton trousers with a drawstring waist. Fauve however, was back in black – a figure-skimming silky dress that ended just an inch or so above the knees – whereas Randi was in his customary blue denim. And Lettie was wearing a shiny silver T-shirt, teamed with a black suede A-line skirt that just skimmed the tops of her narrow thighs.

'How did you fare at juggling, my sweet?' Ivan asked Danni across the table.

Glancing at Al first, she grinned at him. 'OK, I

think,' she replied, 'I kept dropping them at first but Al is such a bully I had to get it right in the end.'

'Good thing too. You keep this lady hard at it, Al,' Ivan said, smiling at them both.

Al laughed a toned-down version of his deep rumble and said, 'Trust me, Ivan, I won't let this little cutie get away with anything. Not even when she turns her big baby blues on me.'

'They're green, actually,' Danni countered, grinning.

As though she were at a tennis match, Danni found her gaze darting back and forth from Ivan to Al, who proceeded to discuss her attributes and her failings as though she wasn't there. She didn't mind. Most of their derogatory comments were mere teasing and they both had plenty of nice things to say about her to counteract the negatives.

It had been agreed that, with the next show only a week away, Al would take over some of Danni's instruction. And, to be honest, Danni thought to herself, she didn't mind at all. She was really beginning to take to the hunky American. Although 'fancy him' might have been a more accurate description. The total opposite of Ivan in every way, he nevertheless had a certain presence that was growing on her in leaps and bounds.

Her reverie was interrupted by the arrival of Guido. At the sight of him in his formal black and white attire, complete with bow-tie, she stifled a smile. He looked like a cross between a typical head waiter and a mafia gangster. So much so that she almost expected to glimpse the outline of a shoulder holster under his jacket.

When he leaned over her to serve her some crisply roasted potatoes cooked with onions and herbs, Danni caught a strong whiff of Giorgio by Armani. This competed heavily with the delicious aroma of the main course which was a very pungent osso bucco. As Guido straightened up and moved away from her to serve Fauve, Danni turned to Al and wafted her hand under her nose while rolling her eyes meaningfully.

Laughing, Al put his arm around her shoulders, drawing her to him. As he put his mouth to her ear he whispered covertly, 'Don't knock the poor guy, he's as nervous as hell.'

As he released her again, Danni straightened up and glanced over her shoulder at Guido, feeling a surge of compassion for the young Italian. Why shouldn't he feel nervous? she asked herself. Just because he was a man didn't mean he should automatically feel more confident about his sexuality than any of the women in the room. Her perception surprised her. For too long, she realised, she had always thought of men as creatures from another planet. Now it struck her that they were only people, with the same hang ups and insecurities as any woman.

'Thank you, Guido,' she said softly, when he returned to her side a few minutes later to pour her a glass of burgundy, 'By the way, you look absolutely gorgeous tonight.'

He flashed her a dark-eyed smile of gratitude.

173

'Really?' he said in a low voice so that the others couldn't overhear him, 'I feel so self-conscious in this.' He pulled at the jacket and grinned ruefully. 'I tell Fauve she try to turn me into a *pinguino*.'

Danni laughed. 'I take it that means penguin?'

'*Si*,' Guido replied, his pearly teeth flashing brilliantly against the canvas of his olive-toned face, 'but Fauve, she tell me not to be a silly boy.' The admission was followed by a self-deprecating shrug.

The image of Fauve saying this which, Danni guessed, had resulted in a smack on Guido's tight backside, made her grin inwardly.

'She is not a lady you can argue with,' Danni confided in him. 'I should know.'

She remembered how Fauve had insisted on shaving her bikini line and felt a small flicker of arousal. There was something about the older woman's dominant air that excited her, she realised. Tiny, she might be, but Fauve had the confidence and awe-inspiring presence of an amazon. No wonder *Cirque Erotique* was such a success. Only an exceptional person could conceive of the idea and then put it into practice with such flair and enthusiasm. An enthusiasm that, Danni suspected, never waned.

Her sudden admiration for the petite Frenchwoman made Danni turn to her and give her an affectionate smile.

'I just want you to know how much I've enjoyed my stay here so far,' she said.

To her surprise, Fauve looked inordinately

174

pleased. 'Thank you, *ma chérie*, she responded, bearing an expression of genuine delight. 'It is good to be told I am doing things right.'

Impulsively, Danni reached out and covered Fauve's hand with her own for just for a brief moment. 'Oh, you are,' she said warmly, 'you're a genius.'

The Frenchwoman laughed and clapped her hands with delight, immediately repeating what Danni had just said to everyone else. It came as no surprise to Danni that they all agreed effusively. Then, by unspoken agreement, they all decided it was time to stop talking and start enjoying the delicious meal instead.

For a change, after dinner the small gathering retired to the huge white on white sitting-room to enjoy coffee and Calvados. Danni sat nursing a huge balloon glass. She swirled the amber liquid around the smooth sides of the glass and occasionally took a tentative sip. Unused to drinking brandy, she found it went straight to her head, even on a full stomach.

Replete with good food and bonhomie she felt herself relaxing further into the squashy sofa. Her eyelids felt heavy, her whole body limp with drowsiness. Ivan came and sat next to her, his hand massaging her bare thigh as he talked to her about the forthcoming *grande performance*, as he called it. It was only a week away and he told her that some very prominent people in international business and government circles had already booked to attend.

175

'What are these people like?' Danni asked. 'Are they perverts or something?' It was a question she had been longing to ask.

She couldn't help wondering if she had over-stepped the mark but Ivan's instant laughter filled her with relief.

'Not perverts, my darling Danni,' he said, 'these people are aesthetes.' He turned to look her straight in the eye and took her hands, cradling them between his long, artistic fingers. 'I think you still do not understand the true nature of *Cirque Erotique*,' he continued. 'It is a unique conception. Artistic. Erotic. Think of the skilled, beautiful people you have met already. And there are others just like them. All dedicated to their art and to self-expression.'

'Will I have to make love to all of them?' Danni asked, surprising herself. It was another question that had been bothering the life out of her but she hadn't meant to actually ask it.

Again, to her relief, Ivan shook his head, though his laughter was gentler and his tone compassionate and full of understanding. 'I have told you before, Danni, the performances are similar to ballet and it is, after all, a proper circus. You seem to have the idea that Fauve and I are planning an orgy of some kind. This is not the case, although—'

'What?' Danni interrupted. She gazed back at him wide-eyed.

Behind her ribcage her heart was thumping and she could feel a mixture of anticipation and sexual excitement coursing through her veins. Her chest

176

felt tight, her throat similarly constricted, whereas the rest of her body felt liquid with desire.

He smiled gently and stroked his hands up her arms. 'I was going to say that after the performances, some people feel the need to take things further.'

'In what way?'

Danni felt she already knew the answer but needed to alleviate the mesmerising effect he was having on her. His voice, so low and rhythmic, was hypnotic in itself. And the caress of his hands on her arms, although innocent, was indescribably arousing, stoking the fire of her passion for him.

Just at that moment Lettie bounded over to them with the grace and exuberance of a puppy – a red setter, Danni decided as she watched her long hair fly. She plopped herself down beside Ivan. Although not unwelcome, her arrival succeeded in breaking the spell between Danni and Ivan completely.

Ivan turned to her. 'Danni was just asking me what usually happens after one of our special performances,' he said.

Lettie laughed and tossed her hair over her shoulder. 'Free love,' she declared gaily.

Danni blanched. So it *was* an excuse for an orgy then.

'Only if you want to though,' Lettie added, when she noticed Danni's look of apprehension. Then she giggled and added with an expansive gesture, 'But usually *everyone* wants to.'

After a few minutes Lettie got up and wandered

away again. Then Ivan was summoned to Fauve's study to take another telephone call. Left to her own devices, Danni indulged herself in a spot of people-watching.

On the other sofa, at right angles to her, Guido was seated between Fauve and Rose with Randi sitting on the arm of the sofa on Fauve's left side.

The two women were talking to Guido, their hands massaging his thighs as they spoke. It was obvious to Danni, by their body language, that between them the two women were seducing the young Italian. Randi was watching intently, his eyes never straying from Guido's face, Danni noticed. All at once Danni found herself thinking, he fancies Guido! The surprising perception leaving her feeling oddly aroused.

Never before had she found the idea of male homosexuality a turn on. But, seeing the yearning expression on Randi's face, and understanding that Guido was unwittingly being prepared by the two women for a new experience, gave her an undeniable thrill. It made a change, for once, not to be the object of everyone's attention herself. And it was then she discovered, with startling clarity, that she wasn't the only one who had something to learn about their sexuality.

When Ivan returned to sit beside Danni again, he found her leaning on the arm of the sofa, her chin cupped in her hands as she regarded the four people on the other sofa with a rapt expression.

'Like a lamb to the slaughter,' she murmured without shifting her gaze.

Ivan laughed throatily and she felt his hand slide up her thigh. 'Prude,' he teased. Just at that moment his hand encountered her bare buttock and he added, 'Hang on, I take that back. You, young lady, are not wearing any panties, are you?'

This time she did turn her head. Her cheeks were pink as she smiled coyly at him. 'I wondered how long it would take you to find out.'

By midnight the atmosphere in the expansive sitting-room had changed considerably. Charged with sexual tension, it now provided the setting for the sort of scenario that Danni had been worrying herself about for days. Only she wasn't worried any longer. In fact, she was surprised to discover just how much she was capable of enjoying.

Inflamed by the discovery of her naughty secret – his words – Ivan had proceeded to caress and arouse Danni to such a degree that she hardly offered any protest when he began to make love to her right there on the sofa. Gradually Lettie had drifted across the room to ask politely if she could join in. After only a moment's hesitation, Danni had invited her to join them. She was lying full length on the sofa with her dress pushed up under her armpits and her thighs splayed wide with Ivan kneeling between them.

He caressed her lower body gently, a couple of fingers pushing deeply into her vagina while he stroked her clitoris with his thumb. He had slipped his other hand under her buttocks and now gently massaged them as he concentrated on arousing her.

Danni expected Lettie to start stroking her bared breasts and was eager for her to start doing so, even arching her back provocatively as an open invitation. So her surprise was mingled with a little disappointment when the young redhead opted to kneel behind Ivan and unzip his fly. His cock filled her tiny hands and Lettie began stroking it eagerly to even greater hardness, while all Danni could do was watch and simultaneously take her own pleasure.

Once again she surprised herself by becoming aroused by the sight of Ivan's cock in Lettie's hands. She watched one slim white hand delve into his trousers to cup his balls and felt an answering frisson of desire.

On the other sofa, Fauve and Rose were busy disrobing Guido who, by the expression on his face, was transported into another realm of ecstasy. Meanwhile, Randi was caressing himself, his stubby cock turgid in his broad hands. A moment later he offered his cock to Guido's open mouth and, after only a moment's hesitation, the young Italian man accepted the ample offering between his lips.

'Oh, God!' Danni grunted.

She couldn't help it. The sight of that cock, dark-skinned with a helmet of livid purple, disappearing into Guido's insolent pink mouth was too arousing. The release of her pleasure was beyond her control. Passion surged through her and, as she watched Lettie's hands working furiously on Ivan's cock, and felt the warm spurt of his semen on her belly, she came with an even louder groan and a frantic churning of her hips.

Until that moment Al, who had merely been a voyeur, walked over to the sofa and gently motioned to Ivan to move out of the way. He grasped Danni by the waist and pulled her up into a sitting position on the edge of the sofa. Lettie obligingly unzipped his jeans and he wriggled out of them. Underneath the jeans his tanned body was naked, his belly washboard flat and his cock impressive in its dimensions.

It reminded Danni of a salami – fat, brown and mouth-wateringly delicious. Avidly, she wet her lips, her hands reaching out automatically to enfold him. His cock felt like a solid rod of muscle and she could feel it twitching with excitement, the blood surging through the prominent veins. Glancing up at Al's face, she asked him to stand in front of her. When he did so, she opened her mouth and fed his cock in inch by delectable inch.

Naked now, Lettie moved to sit behind Danni. Her slim legs slid around her hips and Danni could feel the softness of the young woman's pubic hair as it brushed her buttocks. Whimpering with pleasure Danni felt Lettie's hands rubbing her back and shoulders, then her sides and finally the eager, aching globes of her breasts. With her mouth full of Al's cock, one hand gripping his thigh, the other cupping the heavy weight of his scrotum, she felt her desire mount all over again.

'Beautiful, Danni,' Ivan crooned, stroking her hair. 'You make me so proud, so happy.'

His cock, still rigid, stroked her cheek and she felt a drop of semen streak her skin. Her hand left Al's thigh and reached up to caress Ivan instead. It was the first time she had handled two cocks at once and the very lasciviousness of it made her feel suffused with voluptuous abandon.

Al didn't come in her mouth but urged Danni and Lettie at the last moment to caress each other's breasts while his hot fluid jetted all over them. And she was so wrapped up in the moment that it didn't occur to Danni to demur against his suggestion. Her hands cupped Lettie's tiny, uptilted breasts quite naturally and it was only as she felt the exquisite rosebud nipples between her fingertips that she suddenly became aware of what she was doing.

To hell with it! she thought, tossing aside her natural reticence. This was fun – all of it. Nobody was being hurt or shamed by what was taking place. And everyone was over the age of consent. Why not simply abandon her old inhibitions and go with the flow for a change? With her breasts smeared and tacky with semen, Danni put her arms around Lettie and pulled her close. Their naked bodies meshed, bare breasts – one pair golden brown, the other ivory and rosy-tipped – meeting, flesh on flesh. A moment later Danni experienced her first kiss with another woman.

Their lips met, soft and succulent, opening naturally to exchange sweet, feminine breath. Then their tongues, red darting spears of pleasure, stroked and jostled within the wet cavern of their joined mouths. Danni brushed the sensitive tip of her tongue along the juicy inner flesh of Lettie's lips, quivering to the young woman's answering caress. Poignant and achingly delicate, the bliss of their embrace was without parallel.

'Let me go down on you, Danni,' Lettie begged, when they finally pulled apart. 'You've got such a lovely cunt I want to taste it.'

To know that that sweet mouth was capable of producing such crude words only served to heighten Danni's arousal. She felt the jangling of indecision mingle with the pure white fire of indecent desire. Feeling only the merest flicker of apprehension, Danni waited as Lettie stretched herself out on the sofa. Then she knelt obediently, her knees either side of Lettie's head, with her sex positioned over the young woman's wet, pouting lips.

'Lick her too, sweetheart,' Ivan urged. He caressed her bottom and whispered in her ear. The warm breath on her neck was almost as tantalising as the fingers stroking the cleft between her buttocks and the tongue flickering over her throbbing clitoris.

Still, Danni shook her head weakly. 'I can't,' she said in a hoarse whisper, despairing of the prudish rein that still held her back. But even as she spoke she noticed how beguiling the little nest of red curls looked as they nestled between Lettie's pale thighs. Her pubic hair was quite fine and Danni could make out the pouting pinkness of her vulva. The twin lips of her outer labia had parted slightly to reveal the blushing wrinkly folds of her inner flesh. And when, in the next moment, Lettie drew her knees up and let them fall apart wantonly, Danni saw how her vagina streamed with moisture.

'Taste her,' Ivan crooned in her ear, 'try her sweetness for yourself.'

Allowing her arms to take her weight, Danni placed her hands palm down either side of Lettie's hips. The fleshy bloom of the young woman's sex beckoned to her. She lowered her head tentatively, her eyes feasting on the sight of the juicy, blushing flesh. After a moment the need to touch and explore overcame her. Resting all her weight on one palm, she used the fingers of her other hand to stroke the young woman's mound in an experimental way. The hair was soft and springy and the flesh beneath warm to the touch. Her hand slipped between Lettie's legs, the middle finger easing neatly down the slit between her parted labia. Almost of its own volition, it slid into the wet opening of her vagina.

Lettie, moaned and raised her hips slightly, encouraging Danni to explore her more deeply. At the same time her tongue flickered with increasing rapidity over and around Danni's clitoris. Danni felt her breath catch as her senses soared and her lower body became molten with desire. The hard bud of her clitoris seemed to swell even more as Lettie's tongue drummed rhythmically upon it, as though begging the young redhead to give it even more attention.

Fingers were stroking over Danni's sex. She didn't know who they belonged to, though she assumed they were Ivan's. In the next moment she heard him remark to Al about how wet she was. His insolent comment nearly drove Danni to distraction and she found herself sinking another finger into Lettie's hot, wet chasm in response.

More fingers were now holding Danni's sex wide open. Barely coherent with lust, she could feel warm breath exciting the sensitive flesh around her vagina and then a tongue diving into it like a tiny cock. Her protests emerged from her lips as desperate whimpers. Her capacity for pleasure knew no bounds, it seemed.

In the next moment, Fauve came over to kneel beside the sofa. She cupped Danni's dangling breasts in her hands and kneaded them gently but firmly, like dough.

'Pretty, pretty girls,' Fauve said in her light, accented voice, 'you like Fauve to play with you, no?'

I don't care who plays, just don't stop until I come, Danni pleaded inside her head. Her desire exploded in an anguished moan and she felt her juices flooding out of her.

'Delicious,' Al said, 'the purest honey, from a pure honey bee.' And it was then Danni realised that it was his tongue which probed inside her desperate vagina.

'Fuck her, Al,' Fauve commanded gently.

As she turned her head her lips brushed Danni's shoulder, causing Danni to quiver with delight. And the command in itself was a thrill. It sounded so lewd and yet the thought of a stiff cock inside her greedy body excited Danni beyond reason. Eager to encourage him, Danni wiggled her hips.

'Uh, keep still,' Lettie grumbled from between her legs.

Danni almost laughed but she felt too full of arousal and in the next instant her breath was snatched away as she felt Al's cock plunging into her. Unable to support herself on one hand any longer, Danni resumed her all-fours position. To make herself more comfortable she lowered her upper body so that she was resting on her forearms. With her mouth now positioned conveniently over Lettie's sex, she put out her tongue and licked the pink flesh experimentally.

It tasted good. Sweet, like honey, just as Al had described, yet with a musky, slightly salty aftertaste. Lettie's juices were quite different to the flavour of her own, Danni mused as she lapped greedily at the quivering flesh, yet just as delicious. The young woman bucked underneath her as Danni buried her face further between her legs. Her mouth was full of Lettie's dear, sweet flesh now and when she raised her head just for a moment to catch her breath, Danni was aware that her mouth and chin were dripping with the redhead's nectar.

She was grateful that Al thrust only gently, she didn't want to stop enjoying Lettie and was determined to maintain a certain rhythm that she knew would lead to orgasm. Sucking delicately on the young woman's clitoris she ran the tip of her tongue over the sensitive little pearl at its tip. Lettie bucked her hips convulsively and cried out. All the while, Fauve murmured a litany of encouragement and approval.

'So beautiful, so wet,' the Frenchwoman breathed softly, *'les filles sont incroyables.'*

Danni didn't understand all that the Frenchwoman said but her mind, in any case was elsewhere. Between Lettie's legs. Between her own legs where Al still filled her and Ivan's fingers had taken over from Lettie's tongue. The young woman was too suffused with her own pleasure to continue, Danni realised.

A moment later Fauve and Ivan swapped places and Danni felt the delicate trailing of his fingertips over her fiery breasts and nipples and following the length of her spine. The occasional soft scrape of a fingernail on her labia told her that Fauve was now stroking her clitoris. She manipulated it well, as only another woman could, stroking around and around the desperate bud. The extent of Danni's arousal felt intolerably exciting. She heard muted whimpers and knew they were her own.

When she came, a moment later, so did Al. He had no option. Danni's spasming vagina gripped him, her grasping muscles milking him of every drop. And then a moment later Lettie cried out and slammed her sex up against Danni's face, momentarily smothering her. Her clitoris swelled as though it would burst, then receded under its protective hood as her rigid thighs and clenched buttocks gave way to a gentle quiver.

All three collapsed exhausted and Danni's last impression before drowsiness overcame her, was of Guido's beatific expression as Randi drove into him from behind.

Chapter Ten

DRAGON FLAMES OF red and orange flickered around the bulbous head of the metal rod and painted a sunset reflection on the white canvas wall of the circus tent.

'Careful,' Danni warned Ivan, unnerved by the casual way he waved the flaming rod around, 'we don't want to burn the whole place down at this late stage.'

'Don't panic, it's perfectly safe,' Ivan said with a smile that battled with the flaming rod for intensity and warmth. 'Al often juggles with these you know.'

'I don't doubt it,' Danni replied, pursing her lips in a wry smile. 'That man is an American comic book super-hero come to life.'

It was Thursday morning, with only two days left to go before the grand performance. Trying to play down her feelings of nervous anticipation, Danni was determined to concentrate on the business in hand. Which, on this bright and sunny day, was fire-eating. The rod in Ivan's hand was like a gigantic match. It had a long straight stem and bulbous head, which gave a fiery burst at the merest touch of another flame.

'Now, little Danni,' Ivan instructed in a mock patronising way, 'just concentrate and watch me. Take note of how far I put the flame into my mouth. Hear my breath. No, on second thoughts,' he paused and grabbed her hand, placing the palm against the solid wall of his chest, 'feel my breath. Feel how it leaves my lungs.' So saying he leaned his head back and opened his mouth wide.

Fearful of the flame, Danni flinched out of the way as he brought the rod up and held it over his mouth. As he lowered it slowly she heard, and felt, the sharp exhalation of breath which escaped his throat and immediately extinguished the flame.

'There,' he said as he triumphantly withdrew the rod, 'nothing to it. Now you try.'

She tried to demur. No matter how many times Ivan explained the procedure, and despite the simplicity of his instructions, Danni felt certain she would end up, at best, scarring her tonsils for life.

Plenty of saliva and good breathing control were the secrets of fire eating, Ivan had told her. He had demonstrated the necessary breathing technique countless times, his hand pressed to Danni's breastbone to check that she was doing it right. The first couple of times he had done this, Danni had giggled and tried to encourage him to caress her breasts instead of concentrating on the business in hand. But, Ivan could be intractable when he wanted to be, she had discovered. And this was one of those times.

'We will have the opportunity for games later, Danni,' he admonished her gently, treating her to his melting gaze, 'but for now, we work. This is important.'

'Yes, I know,' Danni sighed wistfully. 'OK, let's give it another go.'

She thought she had the breathing right now. The technique necessitated holding a large gulp of air in her lungs, then expelling it sharply from the back of her throat. The puff had to be strong enough to extinguish the flame. If it reached her lips, it would already be too late. The saliva, Ivan also explained, was needed to dampen the flame.

Taking the rod from Ivan's hand, Danni held it nervously, feeling the way her fingers trembled. Her eyes widened as he lit the bulb at the end and it burst into flame. There was no danger of her hair catching fire, as she had previously feared. Danni had scraped it right back off her face and woven it into an untidy plait.

Fauve had offered to redo Danni's hair for her at breakfast but Danni had refused. There was a part of her she still wanted to keep to herself. Fauve might have taken her pleasure from all other parts of her body during the past few days, but her hair, Danni maintained with silent resolution, was entirely her own domain.

Even with her unruly tresses out of the way, Danni still held the flame as far as possible away from her face lest it singe her eyebrows and lashes.

'Don't be frightened of it, Danni.' Ivan counselled her gently. 'You are the mistress of this flame. Remember that. Remember who is in control.'

Right, Danni thought, taking his words very much to heart. I am in charge, so you, Mr Flame, can just go out when I want you to, OK? She felt much better now, having given the instrument in her hand a good talking to.

Breathing deeply for a few moments, she tried to calm the churning panic in her stomach and the rapid beating of her heart. All at once, her lungs felt constricted. Damn it, the air wouldn't go inside them at all!

Ivan moved to stroke the nape of Danni's neck. 'Calm now, sweetheart,' he crooned, 'just be serene and do everything the way I've told you.'

As his words filtered through Danni's ears and into her brain, she felt all her pent-up tension drain gradually from her body. Her shoulders slumped. The knot unwound in her stomach and her lungs suddenly expanded.

Taking a huge gulp of air, she held it and tipped her head back. She wanted to shut her eyes as she brought the flaming tip of the rod down to her face but forced herself to concentrate on it, and on to holding down those deep lungs full of breath. The flame disappeared inside her mouth. She exhaled hard. With one puff it was all over. The flame went out and she withdrew the rod with a beaming smile of achievement.

'Well done, my darling Danni!' Ivan exclaimed.

Taking the rod from her hand, which now trembled with excitement, he threw it to the ground. In the next instant he picked her up off her feet and whirled her around. Then he set her down and composed his thrilled expression into one of total seriousness. 'Now do it again,' he said firmly.

By lunchtime, Danni was as comfortable eating fire as she was eating the plate of sliced chicken and cold roasted peppers which had been put in front of her.

'You're a bit late, you two,' Rose said as she sat down again to finish her own lunch.

'We've been celebrating,' Ivan said without a hint of embarrassment. He ignored the look of amazement Danni flashed at him and Rose's raised eyebrows.

Christ, Danni thought, was nothing sacred! The memory of half an hour ago made her blush. Consumed by success heaped upon success, Danni had encouraged Ivan to take her from behind as she leaned forward over a small stack of hay bales. The encounter had been brief but nothing less than thrilling.

'Did you know you've got straw sticking out of you?' Lettie asked Danni cheerfully as she entered the kitchen through the back door.

As Danni glanced about her person looking for the straw, Lettie walked up to her and removed a long strand which was poking out from under her leotard just above her left hip.

Lettie sat down opposite Danni and began

pleating the golden length of dried grass. 'Heard the news?' she said, glancing at Ivan.

He shook his head. 'What news – an armed raid on the village post office?'

Lettie smiled. 'No, daft thing. I mean the petition.'

Danni, who couldn't help marvelling at the concept of Ivan being described as 'daft' gazed at the young redhead. 'What petition?'

'To stop the circus performances,' Lettie said.

To everyone's surprise, Ivan shot to his feet and slammed his palm down on the kitchen table so that everything on it rattled.

'No!' he exclaimed, his brow creasing with frustration. 'Not again. Where is Fauve?'

'Gone to the bank,' Rose offered. Her skin, normally as pinkly pale as the inside of a radish, blanched even more, Danni noticed.

All at once, it seemed as though a thundercloud had obliterated the strong yellow sun. The interior of the kitchen darkened in direct proportion to Ivan's mood.

'Those imbeciles,' he said venomously, sounding acutely foreign again to Danni's ears, 'they make a mockery of us and of our way of life. What do they know – or care?' He then proceeded to come out with a litany of expletives the like of which Danni had never heard him utter before. Some of them she didn't even understand.

The three young women shared a look of anguish mingled with surprise.

'This is the last straw!' he shouted.

'No, *this* is,' Lettie interrupted, picking up the crumpled length of dried grass from the table. Her sudden smile wavered and she fell silent. Looking sheepish, she dropped the straw, realising that Ivan was in no mood for jokes.

Ignoring Lettie's attempt at wit, Ivan strode to the door. He stopped when he reached it and glanced over his shoulder. His expression was black with anger.

'Tell Fauve I am in her study,' he said to no one in particular. 'I want to speak with her the moment she comes back.'

There were a few minutes silence after Ivan had gone, broken only by the ticking of the clock and the faint, occasional chirping of a bird.

'The bastards always try it on,' Lettie said at last.

'Meaning?' Danni asked.

'Meaning the villagers,' Rose supplied for her sister. 'They don't understand us, you see. They're always trying to find ways of stopping our performances and closing us down.'

'But they can't, surely,' Danni protested. 'What goes on here is private. It's none of their business.'

'In places like this,' Lettie cut in dryly, 'everything that goes on is everyone's business. Our mum used to say you can't even shit sideways without someone finding out about it.'

Danni stared at Rose for a moment. Then she felt her lips twitching. 'What an odd expression,' she said.

After another few seconds of introspective silence, all three of them burst into relieved laughter.

Fauve arrived to find them collapsed over the table with tears streaming down their faces. When she asked what the joke was all about, Rose told her and then gave her Ivan's message.

The Frenchwoman's expression, which had flickered with amusement, now took on a dark hue similar to that of Ivan's.

'*Bordel de Dieu!*' she exclaimed, flouncing out of the kitchen, clearly on the rampage.

Danni and the twins stared after her in amazement.

'If my memory of French crudities serves me correctly, I think our charming hostess just said "fucking hell",' Lettie muttered.

After lunch, and feeling at a loose end since Ivan's untimely departure from their schedule, Danni wandered into the big top to gaze disconsolately up at the trapeze. She was supposed to have been practising up there again that afternoon. Now, she supposed, that would have to wait until the following day.

She was surprised to feel the soft caress of fingertips on her bare arm and gave a start.

'Meah,' she said when she turned around, 'you made me jump. I was miles away.' Despite the fact that Meah was supposed to be a pupil of the circus school, Danni hadn't noticed her in the big top before.

'I saw you come in here, Danni,' the young woman confessed in her softly accented voice, 'and I follow.'

'Oh?' Danni felt lost for words and merely smiled.

After a moment, Meah resumed stroking Danni's arm. 'I like you, Danni,' she said, looking coy, 'I want that we be good friends.' Her thick, dark eyelashes fluttered as she spoke and Danni thought she could detect a pink flush to the woman's olive-hued cheeks.

'Well, yes,' Danni said, trying to sound brisk but amiable, 'I like you too. Of course I want to be your friend.'

'Then you come with me?' Meah invited as her fingers sought Danni's hand.

Unable to think of a good reason not to, Danni shrugged. 'Sure,' she said, feeling slightly bewildered, 'where are we going?'

Their destination, as it turned out, was Meah's room. Very similar to Danni's in decor, it differed in only two ways. The first was that it had a large brass bed instead of a four poster. And the second was that the room was very neat. Danni couldn't help noticing it's tidiness as she glanced around. She sat down while Meah poured them each a glass of wine and her memory instantly flicked back to the way she had left her own room that morning: the bed unmade, dirty clothes in a heap on one of the chairs and her cosmetics strewn across the surface of the dressing-table.

In comparison, Meah's dressing-table looked as though it had just been polished and bore a rank of bottles and little tubs, arranged according to their height so that they ascended from left to right. Her bed looked as though it had never been slept in and there wasn't a discarded pair of shoes, nor spare item of clothing in sight.

'You're a very tidy person, aren't you?' Danni commented as Meah handed her a goblet of white wine. The glass was tinted green, with little bubbles trapped in its twisted stem.

The young woman shrugged her bronzed shoulders. 'I suppose,' she said. 'Why not to be tidy?'

Why indeed? Danni thought as she watched Meah sit down gingerly on the edge of the bed, as though she didn't dare crease the white satin coverlet. There was nothing wrong with being neat apart from the fact that she believed that life was too short to spend cleaning and tidying things away. She liked to think she subscribed to the Quentin Crisp ethic of housekeeping, which promoted the theory that after the first few inches of dust one failed to notice any further accumulation.

'This wine is nice,' Danni said, for want of something better to say. Then, 'Have you been in this country long?'

'Three years,' Meah replied, 'but I come to the circus school for only five weeks including a visit home. To Mauritius,' she added, as though she thought Danni might assume she meant Croydon or somewhere.

Danni nodded, remembering Fauve's excitement at the young woman's return. 'And what have you enjoyed learning most of all here?' she asked.

She was surprised when a devilish glint touched the dark pools of the woman's eyes and her full ruby mouth twitched at the corners.

'Sex,' she said simply. In an expansive gesture she threw her arms wide open, almost spilling her wine on the pristine bedspread. 'I love it, it is my life now.'

A strange, uncomfortable feeling crept over Danni as she gazed in wonder at the young woman's animated expression. There was something so beguilingly innocent about her, yet at the same time she possessed an animal magnetism. Like a sleek, glossy-haired cat, she exuded a primal heat that screamed out carnal desire from every pore. In was in the way she looked, the way she moved, even the way she sat.

Like now, Danni thought, eyeing the way Meah's proud breasts heaved and thrust provocatively against the simple white cotton top she wore. And how her thighs, barely covered by matching shorts, remained loosely crossed, as though prepared to fall apart at any moment. All it would take, Danni mused, was the merest request, or hint of an erotic caress.

Meah was, she decided, sex incarnate. The living, breathing embodiment of all things licencious. Her hair, which tumbled over her shoulders in thick dusky waves, looked as though it had just been mussed up by a lover. Her easy grace was that of someone who had just tumbled out of bed, still half asleep and consumed by erotic dreams. Sensuality swamped her, from her wriggling brown toes and silky limbs, to her sullen mouth and slumberous eyes.

Good God, I think I fancy her! The realisation brought Danni's covert appraisal to an abrupt halt and she lowered her eyes hastily. She pretended to admire the twisted stem of the green glass and traced it with her fingertips.

It was something she had known all along, she thought, but hadn't wanted to admit, even to herself. From that first evening when she had set eyes on the exotic young woman and coveted the sensation of her milky brown nipples between her lips, the desire for Meah had lain dormant inside Danni's subconcious. Even now, Danni could still recall the musky scent of her arousal and the glossy thatch between her slender thighs, where tendrils of curly hair had become coated with her creamy juices. Her sex had reminded Danni of white chocolate on dark, with a succulent oozing of raspberry filling.

Feeling herself suddenly becoming warm Danni pulled awkwardly at the clingy leotard.

'You are uncomfortable in that thing,' Meah observed. 'You take it off, yes?'

'Well, no I—' Danni began, then stopped. For a moment all she could think about was lying naked beside the dusky young woman. Touching those breasts . . . Between those thighs . . . Did she taste as bittersweet as she looked? she asked herself, feeling her heart begin to pound.

To slake her dry mouth, she took a gulp of wine, then placed her glass on the floor. Standing up she slowly eased the leotard off. Feeling strangely unabashed for once she drew it over her shoulders and peeled it down her body until it spilled around her feet. Then she picked her glass of wine up again and walked boldly towards the bed.

Meah's eyes glittered with excitement. Her red lips parted as Danni walked towards her and, just as Danni reached her, she moved forward and flung her arms around Danni's waist.

Danni gasped with surprise as Meah nuzzled between her breasts. Immediately she felt the wet, exploratory flickering of Meah's tongue.

'Yes,' she murmured, capturing handfuls of the young woman's silky tresses, 'oh yes please.'

Ivan found them entwined together on the bed and was immediately entranced by the sight. Two beautiful women. Naked and unashamed, cloaked only by temporarily satiated bliss. He knew both of them well enough to know that their desire would never be fully assuaged.

Danni was a firebrand, every bit as hot and impulsively reckless as the leaping flames which he had taught her to consume that morning. While Meah tended to simmer. She was the calm before the storm, a tropical heatwave of lust and submissive depravity. Fauve had recognised that much in her right from the start. But then, he reasoned, stepping through the open doorway into Meah's room, no one knew women as well as Fauve.

She had taught him much. And taught him well. He had been young and enthusiastic when he first met her. But without the refinement that he now displayed. Through careful, though wholly pleasurable hours of instruction, during those long sex soaked nights in every corner of the globe, the Frenchwoman had taught him how to please her. How to take his time and appreciate the natural sensuality of the human body.

Then she had encouraged him to practise his newfound art on other women. Those less fortunate than Fauve who hadn't ever known what it was like to be made love to properly. He had a black book as thick as the New York telephone directory and a memory that took him back over many, many bodies and grateful, slumberous smiles.

'If you ever grow tired of the circus, my pet,' Fauve had teased him once, 'you could become a gigolo and be paid for your skill.'

He had laughed off her suggestion. Not because it was a ridiculous notion but because the circus was in his blood. Generations of his family had travelled the world: acrobats, trapeze artists, fire-eaters and lion-tamers. Only he had become a ringmaster and at the one circus which held an unequalled cachet among aesthetic circles – Le Cirque Erotique.

'Ivan?' Danni opened one sleepy eye.

'Yes, sweetheart,' he said, moving to sit on the edge of the bed. He stroked her bare shoulder and glanced at Meah. 'You finally came together then?'

Danni giggled at his pun, knowing it was unintentional and giggled still more at his frown.

'You don't mind, do you,' she asked, wondering if she had misinterpreted his expression. To her relief his face softened into a smile.

'No, silly girl,' he said, 'of course not. I am delighted. Meah has wanted you for so long and you have wanted her, I think.'

She nodded gently. 'Yes, you're right,' she murmured, keeping her voice low so as not to disturb Meah, 'but I only realised I desired her this afternoon.'

He smiled. 'Then it was fortunate I was not around.'

Danni lay back, treating him to an uninhibited view of her naked body. 'How did that business with the petition go – did you manage to sort it out?'

'Not yet,' he said, frowning slightly again, 'but Fauve is – as Al would put it – on the case.'

Just at that moment Meah stirred between them and her heavy-lidded eyes fluttered open. If she was surprised to see Ivan there beside her, she didn't show it.

'Hi,' she said, giving him a sleepy smile. 'You join, yes?'

Ivan hesitated, wondering what Danni would think about it but she smiled and nodded encouragingly.

'Oh yes, do,' she said. 'It would be nice to have a man with us.'

'Ah, so that is all I am to you both, is it?' he joked as he stood up and started to take off his clothes.

'Any cock in a storm,' Danni responded cheekily.

She winked at Meah who gave her a sultry, long-lashed wink back.

As she and Meah moved over to welcome Ivan's long lean body between them, Danni couldn't help marvelling at how far she had come in such a short space of time. At the start of her stay at the circus school she would have been appalled at the idea of sharing Ivan with anyone, even though he had been a brand new lover. Now she felt truly liberated. In body and in mind.

The soft caress of Ivan's hair as he moved to nestle his head between her thighs induced a sigh of pleasure from Danni. Twisting her upper body slightly she began to caress Meah, trailing her fingertips lightly over the brown globes of the young woman's breasts and down over the gently rounded belly to stroke the pulpy flesh between her parted thighs.

Gentle moans filled the air, to be carried away on the late afternoon breeze. The curtains, filmy white, billowed into the room from the open window like interested ghosts – spectral voyeurs who were keen to witness what was taking place on the brass bed.

Danni felt suffused with voluptuous abandon. Her erotic thoughts darted and drifted through her mind as the gentle insistence of Ivan's lips and tongue upon her most intimate flesh carried her to her first orgasm.

He turned to Meah then, whispering instructions to her to move onto her hands and knees so that Danni could wriggle under her and caress her dangling breasts. Pressing his mouth to the open wetness of Meah's sex, Ivan heard her moan and felt the trembling in her body. Danni was suckling her breasts he noticed, her mouth full of one juicy nipple and then the other as her hands rhythmically kneaded both silky brown orbs.

When she had had her fill of Meah's breasts, Danni moved to lie under Ivan instead and took his cock in her mouth. Stroking her lips and tongue down the stem, she paused to lap greedily at his balls before returning to engulf him once again.

They moved in harmony. Their bodies changing position and emphasis until all of them had enjoyed at least one orgasm. Then Danni sat astride Ivan and took his penis deep inside her while Meah straddled his head. As if by silent agreement, the two young women leaned forward to clasp each other's shoulders. They kissed, damp tendrils of dark hair obliterating their faces as their mouths meshed.

Heat surged through Danni. Ivan's cock felt deliciously hard inside her. It stroked her velvety walls and glanced tantalisingly off her G-spot. She tasted Meah's gasps of arousal, felt her body squirming under her hands. At one point she glanced down and noticed how Ivan's tongue speared the young woman. Delving right inside her succulent depths, it finally emerged, glistening with her juices.

The sight drove Danni wild and her fingertips sought the throbbing bud of her own clitoris and massaged it frantically. When she noticed that

Meah was watching her masturbate she felt a further surge of pleasure.

'Come for me, Danni,' Meah whispered, her voice hoarse with passion as she clutched at her own breasts and threw her head back.

Frissons of sublime pleasure coursed through Danni. Meah looked beautiful in the throes of voluptuous abandon. Ivan *was* beautiful. And as for herself, Danni felt as sensual and decadent as a siren luring sailors to disaster as she rode Ivan mercilessly.

Joined together in an erotic trio, they bucked and gasped and fondled and licked. And, a few moments later, all three of them came in a tumultuous expulsion of ecstatic groans.

Chapter Eleven

OF ALL THE feelings Danni had experienced during the past couple of weeks, despair hadn't been one of them. Until now. Sitting on the edge of her bed, her melancholy gaze taking in the bright, airy room and its trappings, she felt acutely homesick. Not for the flat in West London to which she was due to return the day after next but for the place she would be forced to leave – *Cirque Erotique*.

It surprised her that in such a short space of time she could have grown so attached to the circus school and its inhabitants. She had always thought putting down roots involved years of living in the same place and seeing the same old faces: the postman, the Asian couple who ran the late-night grocer's on the corner of her road, even Geoff Wilson, the policeman who religiously walked her particular beat. Now, she thought, she knew better. Belonging wasn't about waving at a familiar face across the street, nor exchanging the same old pleasantries with the old lady nextdoor with nine cats and chronic asthma. It involved getting to know people properly, understanding how they ticked, how they might be feeling at any given time. In all her years as an adult she didn't recall ever feeling as close to anyone as she did to Ivan and the others – even Fauve, who was somewhat remote in comparison.

At that moment Rose popped her head through the doorway that opened out onto the farmyard.

'Hey, misery guts, aren't you coming to get some breakfast?' she asked cheerfully. Her smile faltered when Danni shook her head and deliberately glanced away so that Rose wouldn't be able to see the unshed tears glistening in her eyes. But Rose wasn't to be put off. 'Now, what's all this about?' she persisted, coming into the room and sitting next to Danni. She put a consoling arm around Danni's shoulders and hugged her comfortingly. 'What's the matter, it can't be that bad? Nothing really bad ever happens here.'

Danni turned to look at Rose, her eyes registering the pale pointed face, so like her sister's yet with a more pronounced smattering of freckles across the bridge of her nose. It was this that set the twins apart, making it easier to distinguish one from the other, at least at close quarters.

'I'm dreading going back,' Danni admitted, gulping back a sob. She glanced around and as she did so, the tears were jostled from her eyes and slid slowly down her cheeks in fat, wet drops.

'Oh, crikey,' Rose said, 'you are in a bad way. And I haven't even got a tissue.'

At this, Danni sniffed, then laughed and hiccupped all at the same time. Finally she managed a watery smile. 'I know, I'm just being an idiot,' she said, 'I'll get over it.'

Rose sat back a bit and regarded her thoughtfully. 'Maybe,' she murmured sagely, 'or more likely you won't.' She glanced down at her lap, then up again, fixing Danni with a frank stare. Her pale blue eyes were unblinking. 'I think you're one of us,' she said, surprising Danni. 'Me and Lettie felt just like you do now when it was time to leave. That's why we left home and came here. We haven't looked back. Never been happier, not in our whole lives.'

'And Fauve let you stay here?' Danni asked. 'Just like that.'

Pursing her lips, Rose seemed to consider her question for a moment before answering carefully, 'Not exactly just like that. She gave us both the third degree, I can tell you. Proper put us on the spot she did, wanting to know why we really wanted to stay, as though the relaxed atmosphere and the feeling of being surrounded by really good friends wasn't enough.'

'Was it enough for Fauve?' Danni knew those were exactly the same reasons why she wanted to stay. Somehow, she felt, for a realist like Fauve, they would prove an inadequate explanation.

'Not exactly,' Rose admitted. 'She really kept on digging until we had dredged up all our feelings.'

'And those were?' Danni prompted.

At that, Rose chuckled. 'Well, I'm not going to

tell you, am I? You might come out with the same reasons. The trouble is, if you're only echoing someone else you're not going to sound very convincing.' She paused then added, 'One thing I can tell you, Fauve is a real sucker for sincerity. If she believes you – and believes *in* you – then she'll be your friend for life.' She gave a deep sigh and then stood up, pausing only to plant a gentle kiss on Danni's cheek. 'Why don't you talk to her,' she suggested. 'It can't hurt.'

For a moment Danni felt as if her own private sun had come out again. Then, just as quickly, a cloud of apprehension drifted across it. What if Fauve didn't want her to stay? Danni wasn't even sure if the Frenchwoman liked her all that much. Maybe she was even a little bit jealous of her relationship with Ivan. Danni was a beginner in every sense of the word and not particularly skilled at any of the circus arts which she had learned. Supposing Fauve simply thought she wasn't worth the effort?

'I will talk to her,' Danni said resolutely to Rose. She stood up and walked into the bathroom to blow her nose before coming back into the pretty bedroom. Glancing around, she took the young woman's arm in a friendly gesture. 'Come on,' she muttered, dragging her towards the door, 'the condemned woman must eat a hearty breakfast first.'

Danni tracked Fauve down to her study. It was the first time she had been there and was surprised to discover how different it was from the rest of the rooms in the farmhouse.

Instead of stark, modern simplicity, Fauve's study was a cosy blend of old and new. Antique tables of burnished walnut and mixed wood marquetry stood cheek by jowl with high-backed metal sculpted chairs – like thrones – and steel filing cabinets. The *pièce de résistance* – as Fauve would have described it herself – was her desk. It was a delicate confection of black Chinese lacquer. The modesty panel at the front depicted a typically Chinese scene of a temple and various figures in traditional costume. And the glossy top of the desk bore the incongruous accessory of a word processor.

Seated behind the desk, in a metal and black leather chair, was the enigmatic woman herself. She wore a pair of half-moon glasses perched on the tip of her elegant little nose and she was flicking through the pages of a weighty personal organiser. Covered in black leather, it conveyed the impression that it's owner was a very efficient and popular person.

'I – I did knock,' Danni explained hesitantly, when Fauve glanced up.

The Frenchwoman appraised her silently over the rim of her glasses and motioned to Danni to sit on one of the high-backed chairs opposite her.

'Is there something I can do for you, *ma chère*?' she said, closing the personal organiser and reclining back in her chair. She took off the glasses and placed them on the top of the desk, then sat back again, crossed her legs and clasped her knee with both hands.

'I don't know where to start,' Danni admitted, feeling distinctly uncomfortable.

She found herself staring at Fauve's long red fingernails and wished she hadn't come now. And yet, she told herself firmly, if she didn't take the chance now she would never forgive herself for the missed opportunity.

'Try at the beginning,' Fauve encouraged her with a gentle smile.

Speaking hesitantly at first and then becoming bolder, Danni repeated everything she had told Rose that morning. Just as Rose had said she would, the older woman asked her to describe her real feelings. And Danni did, the words just gushing out before she even had a chance to think about them.

'I just can't bear the thought of going back to my old life,' Danni finished, somewhat lamely she thought, after her outpouring.

'Everything has changed for me since I came here. I'm not the same person any more.'

Fauve was silent for a long time and Danni hardly liked to rush her when she was obviously thinking. With her head turned towards the window she seemed to be gazing at an unseen place, far beyond the boundaries of the front gates and the lane beyond.

While Fauve pondered Danni's dilemma, Danni concentrated on stroking the ears of Delilah, the black labrador. As though grateful for the young woman's undivided attention, Delilah rolled her eyes and settled her chin more comfortably on Danni's lap.

'She likes you,' Fauve said, turning back to Danni and smiling.

Danni nodded wordlessly. Yes, she thought, but is that enough reason to let me stay here?

Presently, Fauve let out a sigh and stood up. She walked to the window and turned, perching her neat jeans-clad bottom on the sill. Then she folded her arms and gazed thoughtfully at Danni. She was wearing the same outfit that she had worn to greet Danni the first day she arrived.

'I do not know what to say to you, *ma chérie*,' Fauve said at last.

Danni groaned inside, desperation gnawing at her. This was it then, this was the big heave-ho.

'But,' the Frenchwoman added, smiling again, 'I 'ave the feeling I should not just say no. I think we need to consider this, you and I. And Ivan,' she said, almost as an afterthought. 'I must ask him what he thinks about all this.'

'He doesn't know,' Danni said quickly. 'I wanted to speak to you first.' She couldn't help noticing Fauve looked surprised.

Then I think it is best if I talk to him first,' the older woman said, 'after all, he is my partner.'

Danni left Fauve's study feeling no more secure about her future than when she had entered. When she met up with Ivan in the big top he couldn't help remarking how worried she looked. To her relief, he seemed to assume that her concerns were about the forthcoming performance.

'I think we will not practise this morning,' he said, taking her arm and steering her towards the exit. 'Al will be here this afternoon to put everyone through their paces but for now we will relax and watch a little film.'

'A film?' Danni's eyes widened in surprise. 'What is it about?'

For the first time since breakfast she felt herself relax as Ivan's warm smile drifted over her. 'The circus, of course,' he said. 'What else?'

If only all cinemas could be as comfortable and as intimate as this, Danni thought as she relaxed further back into the sofa. They were seated in the sitting-room – the only room in the farmhouse that had a TV and video – its hugeness made intimate by the drawn curtains which blocked out the rest of the world.

The video film which they were watching was a complete history of the circus, from its origins in 421 BC, when Socrates was entertained by a troupe of entertainers, and later, in the first century AD, by which time trained animals had started making an appearance. It took them to every country in the globe, depicting various acts and some amazing performers and pieces of equipment.

Danni was particularly taken by a young man named Elvin Bale, who was noted for his skills on the trapeze and had performed with the Ringling Barnum Circus.

'Watch how he does this,' Ivan urged her. He

leaned forward and grasped her knee absently while the television screen flickered with the black and white film. 'Don't blink or you'll miss it,' he added on a cautionary note.

Danni kept her eyes glued to the screen obediently and gasped with amazement as the young man plunged forward from a swinging trapeze and then caught himself by the heels.

'Sensational!' she exclaimed, wide-eyed with delight.

Ivan turned his head and smiled. 'I thought you would enjoy this,' he said. Then he turned his attention back to the film. 'Now watch. This piece of apparatus is called the Whirling Wheel.'

The Whirling Wheel, Danni noted, was a giant wheel of metal and mesh which could spin and revolve at the same time. The contraption was no match for the fearless Elvin Bale, who walked and balanced on it with more grace than the average person on terra firma.

The next scene showed another performer, the unfortunately and inappropriately named Fatini, at the Tower Circus in Blackpool. His act involved something that looked like a street lamp, upon which he balanced on his hands, while the incredibly tall, thin pole swayed dangerously from side to side like a reed in a gale.

Danni was no less impressed by the performers whose acts involved trained circus animals and, by the time the film came to an end, she had temporarily forgotten her despondency. Instead her jade green eyes were glowing when she finally

215

sat back and smiled a thank you at Ivan.

'I feel so inspired,' she said to him while they waited for the video to rewind. 'Right now I could go into the big top and fly like a bird on the trapeze, juggle ten clubs at once and do a hundred backflips.'

'I don't doubt it,' Ivan said, smiling back at her. 'You're a natural, Danni.'

'I am?' She stared at him in amazement.

No one had ever told her that before. Apart from her parents perhaps, who had often commented that she was a natural disaster area. It was then she decided to confess to him her desire to stay, despite knowing that Fauve wanted to speak to him about it first.

'Ah,' he said enigmatically. He looked, Danni thought, quite unsurprised by her admission. 'That explains why Fauve asked me to join her for lunch in private. You have spoken to her about this, I take it?'

'Yes,' Danni said, feeling all her old doubts returning at the mention of Fauve, 'but she didn't look too keen.'

Ivan laughed then and pulled her into his arms. He stroked her hair and shoulders in a comforting, non-sexual way and Danni felt about three years old again.

'Fauve is not the sort of woman to look keen, as you put it,' he told her. 'She prefers to remain inscrutable, like a Chinese Mandarin. But I know she likes you and is very pleased by the way you have settled in here. It is not for everyone.'

'I love it here,' Danni said earnestly, 'the people are so wonderful and friendly. And then there's—' she broke off hastily.

'Yes?' he prompted.

Biting her bottom lip, Danni hesitated. 'I was going to say then there's you, but to be honest I think it's more than that. I feel so free here. I've done things I never dreamed of doing before. And I don't just mean circus things,' she added, blushing.

'I understand, sweetheart,' Ivan said, dropping a kiss on the top of her head. He turned his wrist to glance at his watch. The chrome dial showed it was almost eleven o'clock. 'You must go, Danni,' he said with more urgency and gently easing her away from him. 'Al wants you all to rehearse today and I must try to appease the village idiots. The last thing we need tomorrow night is a petition-waving delegation gatecrashing our performance.'

'Do you think it could come to that?' Danni asked, alarmed. She suddenly had visions of herself involved in some sort of erotic situation and being besieged by photographers from *The Sun* and the *News of the World*. Christ, it didn't bear thinking about, her parents would go spare! She blanched visibly.

'Not if I can help it,' Ivan assured her as he stood up.

His manner was brisk now and Danni decided to make a tactful withdrawal and let him get on with it. She left him with an uncommonly chaste peck on the cheek and wandered off to the big top to find Al and the others.

She awoke on Saturday feeling as though it were Christmas morning and the last day of the summer holidays all rolled into one. She couldn't wait to take part in the grand performance that night and could hardly contain her excitement every time she thought about it. But knowing it would also be the last time she would be together with everyone in the big top made her feel, in the next instant, dreadfully low. It was a seesaw of emotions upon which she couldn't seem to balance. Oh, to be like Elvin Bale, or the great Fatini, they had known how to keep their equilibrium under far more horrendous circumstances.

After breakfast, Fauve invited everyone into the sitting-room to see their costumes. Danni trailed after the chic Frenchwoman wishing she would turn around and say something encouraging. Since the previous morning no mention had been made about Danni's request to stay. Not even by Ivan, who had spent the whole night in her bed.

They had enjoyed a wonderfully sensuous time, made all the more poignant for Danni who hadn't been able to help wondering if it would be their last. She was under no illusions that, on Saturday night, she would be involved in sexual activity with a variety of people, but couldn't be sure if Ivan would be one of them. And being part of a group certainly wouldn't have the same exclusive eroticism as making love in private.

The pendulum swing of Fauve's hips under a tight black skirt stopped at ten to five as she came to a halt in the open doorway to the sitting-room and stood hand on hip.

Glancing over the Frenchwoman's shoulder Danni allowed her mouth to drop open in amazement. For there in front of them were arranged rail upon rail of brightly coloured clothing. Like jewels, the outfits sparkled on the hangers – amazing confections of Lycra and gauze, some hardly more than a wisp of tinted cobweb.

Fauve started up her pendulum motion again and everyone filed into the room. With expectant smiles on their faces, they waited patiently while the older woman walked over to the rails and began handing out items of clothing to their new owners. Occasionally she held a garment in front of herself – a pair of tangerine harem pants; a gauzy shroud of palest pink; a stretchy body-suit of harlequin colours.

'This is for you,' Fauve murmured, handing Danni one of her outfits.

Danni held it up and considered it carefully. It looked as though Fauve had reached up to the sky and snatched a piece of it with which to fashion this garment. Of the palest blue, streaked with white, it was a short floating dress of the purest chiffon. Although it was lovely, doubt crept easily into Danni's mind. There was no disguising the fact that, when she put it on, the garment would be completely transparent.

'Don't worry, sweetheart,' Ivan whispered in her

ear, 'you will look so beautiful—'

'I can't wear this, not in front of all those strangers,' Danni interrupted him. Ivan had told her that almost three hundred 'invitations' to the grand finale had been accepted.

'Of course you can,' he said placatingly as he ran a thoughtful hand over her buttocks. 'Remember, you will be there to be admired. For your skill as well as your beauty.'

There was no time to argue with him. At that moment Fauve interrupted them, pressing another garment into her hands. This one looked more like a bikini. Made of black satin, it had long slits at the front of each underwired cup and the pants were crotchless. Silver and white sequins edged the slits and Danni realised straight away that they would merely serve to draw attention to those parts of the body which were exposed.

'This is to be worn with the bikini,' Fauve said, handing Danni a black cape.

It was constructed of panels of ebony chiffon and taffeta and fastened around the neck with a sequined collar. The cape also had a voluminous taffeta hood.

'To hide my blushes presumably,' Danni said, unable to stop the comment from slipping out.

Fauve and Ivan exchanged a glance, then they both looked at her.

Danni felt herself reeling from the intensity of their dual gaze and was grateful when Fauve reached out and put a hand on her shoulder. At least it stopped her from falling over.

'We 'ave decided,' Fauve said, 'that if you still want to, you may stay on 'ere.'

It took a few moments for her words to sink in.

'Really?' Danni gasped in amazement, 'Do you really mean it?'

Fauve and Ivan's faces lit up with smiles and the older woman planted delicate, rosebud kisses on each of her cheeks.

'Welcome to *Cirque Erotique*,' she said simply, in a husky voice that sounded choked with emotion. Then she seemed to recover her usual sang froid, turning and clapping her hands together briskly to summon everyone's attention. They all glanced up: Al, Guido, Randi, Meah and the twins, Lettie and Rose. '*Tout le monde*, Danni 'as decided to become the latest member of our *petite troupe estimée*,' Fauve announced in the Franglais that was typical of her and which Danni found so endearing.

A whoop of congratulation went up and, with all the élan of a conjurer, Ivan produced a bottle of champagne. There was a tray of glasses on a black lacquered side table and now he shared the foaming mixture amongst them and handed a glass to each person in the room.

'To Danni,' he said in a simple toast, raising his glass aloft.

'To Danni,' they all chorused.

Glancing around at all of them, Danni felt herself glowing with pleasure. Now, at last, she felt as though she really and truly belonged at *Cirque Erotique*.

A little while later, they all took their costumes
back to their rooms. Al's room was next to Danni's
and so he walked with her across the courtyard,
chivalrously taking command of her costumes.
When they reached her room, she invited him in
for a cold drink.

'That champagne has made me feel thirsty,
would you believe?' she said, laughing.

'Where shall I put these?' Al asked, holding up
her costumes – such as they were, she thought,
taking them from him and hanging them on the
hook on the back of the bathroom door.

She noticed that, for once, he didn't have his
long hair tied back in a ponytail. Instead it fell
down his back in a smooth chestnut curtain.

'I love your hair,' she said impulsively, stroking
it.

'Most women do,' he admitted but without
conceit. Grasping her by the wrist, he held the
palm of her hand to his mouth and kissed it.

Danni felt herself melt. Next to Ivan, Al was the
most attractive man she had ever met.

'Sit down, please,' she said, feeling strangely
flustered, 'I should have offered before.'

His eyes twinkled in his nut brown face. 'I'd
rather *lie* down, with you, honey,' he said in a voice
that was low and filled with promise.

The ache that immediately consumed her body
made Danni feel faint. She reeled slightly and
wondered whether it was purely by accident that

she happened to veer towards the bed as she fell.

She was wearing a pair of shorts and a T-shirt and in moments Al was lying beside her, pushing her T-shirt up, over her head.

Warmth crept over her as stealthily as a cat burglar as Al stroked his broad hand across her bare stomach. Beneath the rose coloured satin bra that she was wearing she felt her breasts swell and her nipples harden. Was this to be her way of life from now on, she asked herself dreamily as he began to pull down her shorts and panties all in one go? What once would have appalled her – the idea of moving from man to man, even man to woman – now seemed as natural to her as breathing.

Sensual exploration combined with erotic gratification was the philosophy of *Cirque Erotique*. Did this mean she now considered sex to be the most important component of her life? Sex and love, she amended mentally. It was inescapable that she loved the others in different ways and felt loved in return. If there was one thing she had learned during the past two weeks, it was that everyone at the circus school respected each other and would never dream of taking advantage.

Everything that had happened to her had been with her consent – whether she had been able to admit it to herself at the time or not. Even when she had been strapped to the board after taking part in Ivan's knife throwing act, she had been the willing victim of the twins. All it would have taken was the simple word 'no' and they would have left her alone. She knew it now and realised she had known it then.

'Dreaming, honey?' Al asked as he moved to kneel between her legs. 'Open wide,' he added, smiling when she did as he asked.

'Thinking,' she corrected him, 'thinking how lucky I am.'

She finished on a gasp as Al spread her outer labia wide apart and ran his tongue down the fleshy slit between them. The silky strands of his hair tantalised the sensitive flesh of her inner thighs and stroked across her belly. Moving easily into the realm of erotic sensation, Danni willingly abandoned all attempts at rational thought for the time being. There would be plenty of time for self-congratulation when she was alone and thoroughly satiated.

Chapter Twelve

EXCITEMENT HUMMED IN the air. The atmosphere, no longer that of a rural retreat, was now one of lavish opulence. Redolent with expensive perfumes, the balmy evening breeze carried with it a strange melée of accented voices, the constant slamming of car doors, the swish of silken coats and dresses and the crunch of footsteps on the gravel path.

Shielded by the curtain, Danni watched the guests arriving, all dressed as if invited to a grand society ball. There were people of all descriptions: tall men in dress suits with willowy blondes on their arms; squat men with bald heads and handlebar moustaches; stout dowagers with throats encircled by diamonds; and arty, eccentric types with ponytails and crushed velvet jackets. Singly or in animated cliques, they streamed into the farmhouse to be greeted by Fauve. Then they would be offered champagne and canapés before being directed to claim their seats in the big top.

The side meadow had been turned into a car

park for the evening and by craning her neck, Danni could make out the gleaming bodywork of Rolls Royces and Mercedes limousines. Such ostentation was interspersed with cars much sportier but none the less expensive, Porsches, Ferraris and Aston Martins being among those that she recognised.

A knock at the door drew her away from the window and she hastened to answer it. She was surprised to see Fauve standing there. Every inch the chic Frenchwoman, she was dressed in a long black sheath of an evening gown which shimmered with sequins and sparkled almost as much as her smile.

'Surprised to see me?' she said, swaying into Danni's room.

Standing back to let her in, Danni nodded dumbly, then said, 'Er, yes, I thought you would be busy with all those guests. I've been watching them arrive.'

Fauve's smile lifted even more. 'It is a wonderful turn-out, *n'est-ce pas*?' She sat in the small chair by the bed and motioned Danni over to her. 'I 'ad to come, to wish you good luck,' she added, sounding slightly breathless, 'you are our protégée after all.'

'Well, thank you,' Danni replied, feeling over-awed at being singled out for such attention when she knew the older woman had a much greater duty to her guests.

Gradually, she came to realise that Fauve was appraising her and in the next instant remembered that she was dressed only in her first costume for the evening – the chiffon dress. Short and floaty it danced around the tops of her thighs when she moved and did absolutely nothing whatsoever to disguise the curves and shadows of her naked body beneath. Immediately, she felt like covering up and her hands fluttered nervously in front of her.

'Don't be shy,' Fauve insisted huskily. She reached out to Danni and slid her palms over her stomach, flattening the gauzy fabric against it and pulling it tightly over the firm globes of her breasts. Her pubic hair snagged the chiffon and was clearly visible as a neat, golden brown triangle. Fauve smiled at Danni's blushes. 'You are so beautiful,' she said, 'you must not be ashamed to show off your body.'

'Me, beautiful?' Danni laughed nervously. Although she had been told the same thing by other people during the past couple of weeks, she still couldn't get to grips with the notion.

Fauve's smile changed to an expression of pure desire. 'Yes, you, Danni,' she said. 'And your beauty is not just on the outside but comes from in 'ere.' She smoothed a thumb over Danni's ribs, just beneath her left breast.

Feeling her breath catch, Danni realised that the reason she felt so unsure of Fauve was because deep down she desired the older woman. And it was only now she understood that she had felt the first stirring of erotic longing the day she spoke to her on the phone. Later, when Danni set eyes on

Fauve for the first time, her feelings had been confirmed. At that point she had been largely ignorant of her own latent urges and what she felt inside had gone unrecognised. Danni hadn't known then what it was like to give full rein to her sensuality and that she could enjoy making love to another woman. Thank God, she mused, that she knew better now.

Kneeling down, Danni stroked her palms up Fauve's slender arms in a tender, exploratory gesture. Then, feeling emboldened by the woman's acquiescence, she leaned forward and pressed her lips to the perfectly formed rosebud mouth that glistened with bold red lipstick.

Fauve's mouth opened naturally under hers and she felt the warmth of the Frenchwoman's body as she pressed against it. The sequins prickled through the thin chiffon and she yielded to the sensation of Fauve's hands roaming her back and sliding up under the hem of her short dress to stroke her bare bottom.

'Ah, my sweet Danni,' Fauve murmured when they broke apart, 'this is so wonderful but it will not do. Not now.' She glanced at her elegant gold wristwatch and shook her head regretfully. 'Later,' she promised in a husky voice, 'after the performance. You and I, we will share our first whole night together.'

Shakily, Danni stood up. Trickles of her own juices ran down the insides of her thighs and her body felt hot and heavy, filled with a voluptuous yearning that needed to be assuaged.

'I'm so nervous,' Danni admitted, watching her fingers pleat the hem of her short dress while her mind whirled with anticipation at what was to come – and what would come later.

'You will put on a brilliant performance, I think,' Fauve said, inspiring Danni with confidence.

She stroked a finger delicately up the inside of Danni's thigh and caught some of the fluid on its tip. Holding it to her smudged lips she tasted it and smiled. Oh, yes, her eyes seemed to say, yes, Danni, we will have such fun from now on. Standing up abruptly she smacked Danni lightly on the buttocks and told her to get her things together and scoot over to the big top. Pausing to take the black satin cape from its hook on the back of the door, she draped it around Danni's shoulders.

'Better to wear this,' she advised with a wicked smiled, 'otherwise my guests, they will ravish you a thousand times over before you reach the big top.'

The thought only slightly disturbed Danni, who shivered, but with excitement rather than apprehension.

'Thank you, Fauve, for everything,' Danni said, wrapping the cape around her and reaching for the bikini which matched it.

Fauve made a tutting sound and seemed to shrug off her thanks. 'Just enjoy yourself tonight,' she said, 'and we will talk again after the show. And now I must go. Take care, Danni and *bonne chance.*'

As Danni stood in the wings of the big top and surveyed the ring, which was filled with familiar apparatus of all descriptions, she felt as though she would need all the luck she could get just to survive the next few hours. Although Ivan and Al had schooled her well and she knew exactly what she must do and when, she still felt horribly nervous. Never before had she performed in front of an audience and could not have imagined putting on a performance such as this – even for a lover and in total privacy.

Her gaze travelled around the banks of seating which had been erected to form a semicircle around the front half of the ring. The plush red velvet chairs were filling up fast. Divested of their coats, the audience now appeared as a shimmering, jewel coloured sea, their faces as bright and animated as their clothing. Each discovered a pair of opera glasses on their seats and Danni found herself trembling as she imagined the close up view they would have of the performers on display – including herself. No part of her would go unmissed that evening. Three hundred pairs of eyes would be able to share in every visual delight her body had to offer.

'Nervous, Danni?' Ivan spoke softly in her ear.

She glanced around and felt her eyes widening, her body responding automatically to his nearness and the splendid sight of him in his ringmaster's costume. Tight white breeches clung to his lean thighs and followed the curve of his buttocks and the intriguing bulge at his groin. Above these he wore a white silk shirt topped by a red tail coat with black velvet lapels. The breeches were tucked into gleaming black leather riding boots and his white blond hair flowed like a mane from beneath the brim of a black felt top hat. The last and most intriguing addition, one which made Danni's stomach clench with a latent desire yet to be explored, was the black leather whip which he held coiled loosely around his hand.

'You look magnificent,' Danni gasped, her eyes rapidly trying to take in the full beauty of him. She could feel her heart beating fast behind her ribs, her body melting. His stature and the gaze he favoured her with was proud and masterful.

'Thank you, darling girl,' he said softly, appearing totally unfazed by her open admiration. 'And you, of course, look beautiful.'

'I do, don't I?' she said, accepting the compliment for once.

In truth, she did feel beautiful. Rose had helped her with her hair, curling it with tongs and piling the resulting corkscrews on top of her head. The style gave her more height and showed off the sweep of her neck and shoulders which, she had been forced to admit, looked achingly lovely and graceful. And she had grown used to the filmy dress she was wearing, hardly minding now that it drew attention to the body underneath rather than disguised it at all. On her feet she wore pale blue satin ballet shoes to match her dress. And she found herself high stepping as she walked, her heels hardly touching the ground as the balls of her feet took most of her weight.

The combination made her feel beautiful and ethereal, like a rather licentious fairy who flaunted and teased as she floated around. This, she was certain, was the effect Fauve had intended to achieve all along. The Frenchwoman was, Danni recognised now with an emotion close to love, a very clever, very remarkable woman and she felt privileged to be one of her chosen few – a fully fledged member of *Cirque Erotique*.

Music filled the big top, drowning out the hubbub of cosmopolitan chatter. It came from a small orchestra which, Ivan had told her, was one of the finest in Europe. Danni couldn't place the composer of the piece they were playing. She only knew a little bit about classical music yet thought she recognised the influences of Tchaikovsky, Wagner and Dvorak in there somewhere.

'We're on,' Ivan murmured softly in her ear. Then he strode past her and out into the middle of the ring.

He stood there for a moment, tall and commanding, his body turning this way and that, surveying the gathering before him with arms outstretched in welcome. Then he turned and cracked the whip. The black leather thong snaked through the air and fell, biting into the sawdust and throwing up a small cloud.

This was the signal for the opening procession and Danni, along with all the others in their

232

brightly coloured, wantonly revealing costumes, immediately painted smiles on their faces and stepped out to meet the crowd. As she circled the ring Danni keenly felt the sensation of all eyes being upon her. Her breasts and bottom bounced as she skipped lightly on tiptoe. Her hairstyle wobbled on top of her head, one silky tendril falling to caress her cheek and shoulder. Instead of running for cover as she would have done not that long ago, she kept proudly in step. Taking the admiration of the crowd as her due, for once she felt, not as the old Danni, but beautiful and voluptuous in the most perfect, feminine way.

As she came full circle, she broke away with Guido and climbed the ladder to the trapeze. A draught of air snaked across her bare buttocks and whipped between her legs as she climbed. She felt acutely aware of the opera glasses trained on her, knowing how much must be revealed as she mounted each rung of the ladder. Her cheeks felt warm, tinted hot pink with spots of shame. Yet at the same time she was enjoying herself. Being the object of attention was wonderful – shamefully titillating yet overwhelming in its glorious flamboyance.

Below her, for she was no longer afraid to look down, she saw other members of the circus troupe engaged in various acts. Lettie and Rose were on unicycles and Danni could easily imagine the sensation of their naked vulvas pressed against the leather saddles, rubbing lightly as they pedalled. They were wearing dresses similar to her own but in a strong shade of verdant green which suited their colouring beautifully.

From the audience came ripples of applause and gasps of admiration. Danni knew that the evening would gradually warm up in terms of erotic content, while maintaining the overall theme of a traditional circus performance. Beautifully choreographed by Al, the troupe tantalised and teased the audience through carefully executed movements and displays. They caressed each other briefly as they moved together and then apart, slowly warming the atmosphere, charging it with undeniable frissons of concupiscent tension.

Aided by Guido, who cast his hand lingeringly over her breasts and between her legs as she moved, Danni climbed onto the trapeze. She swung to and fro, feeling the air current catch the hem of her dress and lift it. A collective gasp ran around the audience below, diverting Danni momentarily. After a moment she regained her composure. Moving gingerly, she allowed herself to drop down, catching the trapeze with her feet and entwining them around it. Her hold was solid, perfectly safe enough for her to let go with her hands and swing upside down.

Above her, Guido walked the tightrope, his body, lithe and swaying like a reed in tight black Lycra which clung to every curve and delineation of his lean musculature. He crossed easily, skipping the last few feet with the natural grace of one born to his chosen art and bounding lightly to land on the small platform. Then he caught the other trapeze, swung himself down to hang upside down like Danni, then swayed towards her.

Back and forth they swung, caressing each other lightly as they came together. On the third swing, Guido caught Danni's dress which hung down now over her face, and pulled at it, dragging it over her head.

Hanging bat-like and completely naked, Danni watched the ethereal piece of gauze float like thistledown to land on the net below. They hadn't rehearsed this, she thought, shocked for an instant by what had happened. But before she could gather her thoughts, Guido was swinging towards her again, positioned on his trapeze so that he could grasp her around the waist and bury his face between her wide open thighs.

She saw the upside down faces of the audience, opera glasses trained upwards, watching intently as Guido held on to her while they swung. His tongue lapped over her exposed vulva and snaked her outer labia apart. It tantalised her clitoris and glided along her slit, rimming her vagina before following the crease between her buttocks. Her cheeks flared with shame. Short of allowing herself to fall there was nothing she could do except abandon herself to the moment.

A short while later, a tumultuous orgasm weakened her grip and sent her tumbling to the ground. The net caught her trembling body and she scrambled to the edge as gracefully as she could, her face and throat flaming. Only the whispered congratulations of Al and Rose, and eventually Guido when he had descended the ladder, prevented her from feeling as though she had shamed the entire troupe.

'Marvellous,' Al said in a stage whisper as he led her, naked and still trembling, from the ring, 'I couldn't have orchestrated that better myself.'

There was no time to ponder her imagined disgrace. Danni had only a few minutes to put on her second costume of the evening. Fauve helped her to dress, sliding the straps of the bra over her shoulders and fastening it at the back. Then Danni stooped to step into the bikini bottoms.

After appearing stark naked in front of the audience, she didn't think she could feel at more of a disadvantage, yet she was surprised to find that in this outfit she did.

'Let me look at you,' Fauve said, turning Danni around so that the two women faced each other. 'Shoulders back, now,' she admonished gently when Danni tried to hunch her body to shield it. 'Let me see those lovely breasts thrusting.'

Danni stifled a nervous giggle. With her shoulders back and head erect as Fauve instructed she could feel her breasts oozing over the cups, the tips of them swelling obscenely through the slits at the front. To her complete mortification, Fauve rubbed her fingertips over the swelling buds of her nipples, exciting them, making them stand out even more.

'I rouge them,' Fauve suggested, producing a pot of blusher as if from nowhere.

Danni bit her bottom lip as the older woman's

fingers rubbed the tinted powder into her nipples. Then she glanced down. Her nipples seemed huge, all swollen and ripe like juicy berries. She stopped biting her lip to run her tongue over it and then over her upper lip.

'Good enough to eat, eh?' Fauve asked, her dark eyes glinting wickedly. 'Now we attend to your pretty little nether regions.'

Before Danni could offer any protest, Fauve sank to her haunches and considered the view that the split crotch offered. She reached out and touched Danni, making adjustments, easing Danni's outer labia apart and covering them with the satin so that her clitoris and inner labia were exposed. The fabric seemed to grip her labia, holding them in the position Fauve favoured. Then the older woman got to work with the rouge again, reddening Danni's slit so that it matched her nipples and the blush that stained her cheeks.

While she did this, Danni groped blindly for something to hold on to. Her legs were shaking so much and her clitoris, still sensitive from the orgasm that Guido had given her, throbbed and swelled even more each time Fauve's fingertips glanced across it. She stroked on the rouge with exquisite precision, circling Danni's clitoris time and time again until she was whimpering with lust. She felt so desperately aroused that, when Ivan appeared and told them that he was about to call Danni into the ring again, she almost pleaded with him for more time.

His knowing glance swept over her body, lingering on her quivering vulva and swollen nipples before reaching her face. He fixed her with his mesmerising gaze, his expression at once lustful and commanding.

'Rude girl,' he admonished, smacking her sex lightly so that he was left with a red stain on his fingertips. 'Plenty of time for that later. You must come out and finish the show, our audience awaits.

Danni knew that this time she and Ivan would be performing together. The round, red and white board awaited her, the leather shackles open and ready to receive her wrists and ankles. Part of the grand finale was to be the knife-throwing act for which Ivan was famed. And Danni was to be his assistant. Spread-eagled and tethered, with the most intimate parts of her body diabolically exposed, the blushing flesh contrasting so acutely with the black satin, she was to appear in front of everyone as a sacrifice.

As she walked out into the ring again, her hand tucked reassuringly in Ivan's, she heard a muted ripple of applause. Then, as she positioned herself in front of the board and two young orientals – one male and one female, who Danni had never met before – stepped forward to enclose her wrists and ankles with the restraints, there was a collective gasp of approval.

She tried to concentrate on the oriental couple and blot out the vision of the sea of faces that surrounded her. The couple were dressed from neck to ankle in closely fitting black bodysuits. The bodysuits matched the colour and silkiness of their hair and had zigzag panels of smoky hued gauze across the torso, revealing a nipple here and the under curve of a breast there, as well as their entire pubic area.

They were both around the same age as her, Danni estimated, and she remembered now that they formed part of a small acrobatics troupe from Korea. The girl was a contortionist and had earlier delighted the audience by bending right over backwards. The position had thrown her barely concealed vulva into lewd prominence and she had managed to peer through her legs at the audience, her expression a mixture of feigned surprise and deliberate naughtiness.

Now Danni felt the caress of their fingers as they fastened the restraints and deliberately explored the length of her limbs. It was all part of the act, although Danni had previously rehearsed it with the twins, Lettie and Rose. Ivan strode over and pretended to shoo the couple away. The young woman cowered from the threat of the whip but the young man had to pretend to challenge Ivan. Keeping his eyes fixed on the stony gaze of the ringmaster, he slid his fingers up the inside of Danni's thigh and right into her vagina.

With a small gasp, Danni wriggled her hips as much as the restraints would allow. It wasn't part of the act but the audience loved her 'pretence' at outrage. Pretending to ignore Ivan, the young man turned to smile wolfishly at the audience, taking orders from them to probe Danni more deeply and stroke her clitoris and nipples.

'No,' Danni moaned, moving her head from side to side, trying to deny the way her body responded of its own accord.

'A virgin sacrifice,' Ivan announced. 'What should we do with her?'

The suggestions that came rebounding back from the audience were wholly licentious. They were also wickedly thrilling and Danni felt herself moving onto a higher plane of eroticism. Never before had she been treated like this, her body exposed to hundreds of voyeurs and made more open and moist by a stranger's exploring fingers.

Now the girl joined in, pinching Danni's clitoris lightly, laughing aloud when Danni moaned with desire. Leaving her throbbing clitoris alone for a moment, her hands moved up to Danni's breasts and she began to play with the nipples, pulling and pinching them until they became fully swollen and distended. She smacked Danni's breasts sharply with the palm of her hand, admonishing her for her naughtiness and lack of control.

'Rude girl,' she scolded, echoing Ivan's earlier sentiment as she slapped them again. But in her accent it came out as 'lewd girl', which was still an accurate description, Danni thought, half laughing, half groaning inside her head.

She felt so consumed by desire and by the shameful pleasure she was deriving from the situation she wondered, fleetingly, if she would ever recover. Ever be 'normal' again – whatever that was.

On the front row of the audience, directly in

front of Danni sat an oldish man, steel-haired and distinguished. Beside him sat an incredibly beautiful woman of around the same age, with a bouffant of pale hair that had obviously faded from golden blonde.

They both looked as if they had plenty of 'old money', Danni thought, trying desperately not to meet either pair of eyes. The woman was clothed in a long red taffeta dress, its luscious folds billowing out, exposing only slim ankles and a dainty pair of feet clad in matching satin shoes. Around her throat she wore a simple three string collar of black opals and similar huge, drop opals hung from her earlobes. She looked exquisite, Danni mused, holding in a gasp as the young orientals stroked and tantalised her yearning sex.

Against her will, she found her gaze drawn to that of the man. He wore a traditional black dress suit and looked immaculate but for his bow tie, the meandering ribbon of which hung from his collar. The top button of his pristine white shirt was undone and just occasionally, she noticed, he moved a finger to his throat, as though the collar was still restricting him in some way.

Realising that it was she who was having that effect on him made Danni feel less embarrassed and more voluptuous still. Fixing his pale grey eyes with her own insouciant gaze she pouted slightly and let out a clearly audible whimper. The man flushed, his finger moving to his collar again, battling against it. His eyes could not stay with hers, she noticed, with only the slightest flicker of shame, but kept dropping to that place between her legs where her flesh throbbed and pouted and streamed with the evidence of her arousal.

What Danni didn't realise was that behind her, beyond the limited scope of her vision, various scenes of similar eroticism were being enacted by the other members of the troupe. But for her and the couple on the front row, it was as if she were the only performer and they her exclusive audience.

Turning her head slightly to look at the woman, Danni noticed how she seemed to be totally involved in what was happening. Her bosom was heaving, her breathing short and rapid and two brilliant spots of pink appeared in her cheeks. Her eyes were over bright, sparkling with excitement and the tip of her tongue darted out with increasing frequency to moisten her wide, rosy lips.

Seeing this, recognising the outward signs of the woman's own arousal, Danni felt her passion mount. She wanted more than anything to offer herself to the couple, to enjoy them as they would surely enjoy her. Yet all that would happen between them would be a meeting of minds and a sharing of visual pleasure.

This was her reward, she realised. This was the reason why *Cirque Erotique* was so successful. It was the perfect combination of fantasy and fact. Voyeurs and performers conspiring to meet in an atmosphere of perfect complaisance. The audience gave their money and their appreciation and the members of *Cirque Erotique* gave their bodies and their voluptuous sensibilities in return.

Able now to embrace the true philosophy of the unique band to which she was forever joined, Danni gave herself up to the glorious sensation of giving and receiving. She arched her back, thrusting her hips forward, offering herself to her tormentors and her audience. Then, with a loud cry of joyous abandon, she came . . . and came . . . and came . . .

Afterwards, when the oriental couple stepped back to allow Ivan to continue with his act, Danni hardly noticed the flashing steel blades which whistled towards her to become embedded in the wood. She felt completely at one with the circus troupe and the audience. And as Ivan helped her to step forward and take a bow at the end of the act, her cheeks were flushed with pleasure rather than embarrassment.

They had only a few minutes to compose themselves before Ivan had to go back out into the ring to announce the finale. Fauve surprised them all again by producing a third set of costumes.

'I did not know if they would be ready in time,' she admitted, 'but my seamstresses from the village, they work like demons.'

The costumes were variations on a theme. White silk and satin, trimmed lavishly with matching feathers. Danni's dress, a clinging white sheath, clung to every curve and was cut so low at the back it showed the upper swell of her buttocks and the first inch or so of the crease between them. It dipped low at the front as well and was slit from ankle to waist, around which a matching belt was fastened at the front with a square diamanté clip.

The stark simplicity of the dress set off her tan beautifully. And when she walked, the silk flowed over her body like single cream. With each step a lean, tanned leg appeared and the slit widened to reveal a tantalising glimpse of her pubis.

'Lovely, *ma chérie*,' Fauve enthused, her face wreathed in smiles as she clapped her tiny hands together delightedly, 'and 'ere is the finishing touch.' So saying, she draped a long white feather boa around Danni's throat so that it trailed down her back, the feathers teasing her bare skin.

Danni pulled back the flap of red and white striped curtain that shielded them from the audience.

'So far so good,' she said, 'we haven't been raided by an angry mob of villagers yet.' Then she clapped a hand over her mouth and stared wide-eyed at Fauve. 'Omigod, I shouldn't have said that. It's tempting fate.'

'No need to worry,' Ivan said as he stepped through the curtain to join them, 'Fauve and I have already sorted that out.'

'How?' Danni glanced from one to the other.

Fauve held up a hand and rubbed the tips of her fingers together. 'Money, my darling girl,' she said with a wicked smile.

'It works every time,' Ivan cut in, 'they soon stopped complaining when Fauve and I offered to donate a share of the takings to the fund for a new village hall.'

'Clever,' Danni said approvingly.

'Philanthropy,' Ivan corrected her, 'is a wonderful thing.'

In the main body of the big top, the orchestra started up again. This time Danni recognised the music as Mahler.

'Our closing act,' Ivan said, 'wait one moment, Danni, I have a couple of friends for you.'

Surprise was written all over her face as he disappeared into the throng of performers behind them. She glanced at Fauve who gave her an insouciant shrug in reply. Moments later he returned and Danni felt her stomach contract with alarm. In each hand he held a short black velvet lead. Each lead was attached to a beautiful diamanté collar. And each collar encircled the graceful neck of a sleek black panther.

'We broke our own rules about not involving animals in the circus,' he explained, passing the ends of the leads into Danni's stunned hands. 'Meet Sheba and Cleopatra.'

'I – I—' Danni felt beads of perspiration break out on her forehead.

'Do not worry, *ma chérie*,' Fauve reassured her, 'they are perfectly tame. They come from the local circus and are only for show.'

'They are far less vicious than this little cat here,' Ivan said, squeezing Fauve's shoulder affectionately.

Danni glanced at Sheba and Cleopatra who gave her a blank, yellow-eyed stare in return. Then Cleopatra yawned sleepily and nuzzled Danni's leg.

'See,' Ivan added with a broad smile, 'friendly as kittens.'

There was no time to argue with him. It was time to go back out into the ring. With Ivan walking proudly ahead, Danni and the others followed. By the time they had walked a few paces to the centre of the ring, Danni felt quite comfortable with Sheba and Cleopatra and the roar of approval that went up as Danni entered, swathed in her white silk and feathers and leading the sleek black cats, was enough adulation to turn any girl's head.

I was born to this, she told herself proudly, as she stood centre stage, flanked by the panthers and surrounded by all the other performers. Her old life seemed a million miles away now. Consigned to a different era. This was a new beginning and, she knew deep inside, the start of a wonderful, sublimely erotic existence.

THE X LIBRIS READERS' SURVEY

We hope you will take a moment to fill out this questionnaire and tell us more about what you want to read – and how we can provide it!

1. About you ...

A) Male   Female

B) Under 21   41–50
                  21–30   51–60
                  31–40   Over 60

C) Occupation_____

D) Annual household income:
                  under £10,000   £31–40,000
                  £11–20,000   £41–50,000
                  £21–30,000   Over £50,000

E) At what age did you leave full-time education?

                  16 or younger   20 or older
                  17–19   still in education

2. About X Libris ...

A) How did you acquire this book?

I bought it myself
I borrowed/found it
Someone else bought it for me

B) How did you find out about X Libris books?

in a shop
in a magazine
other_____

C) Please tick any statements you agree with:

I would feel more comfortable about buying X Libris books if the covers were less explicit

I wish the covers of X Libris books were more explicit

I think X Libris covers are just right

If you could design your own X Libris cover, how would it look?

D) Do you read X Libris books in public places (for example, on trains, at bus stops, etc.)?

Yes   No

3. About this book ...

A) Do you think this book has:

Too much sex?
Not enough?
It's about right?

B) Do you think the writing in this book is:

Too unreal/escapist?
Too everyday?
About right?

C) Do you find the story in this book:

Too complicated?
Too boring/simple?
About right?

D) How many X Libris books have you read?

If you have a favourite X Libris book, what is its title?

Why do you like it so much?

4. Your ideal X Libris book ...

A) Using a scale from 1 (lowest) to 5 (highest), please rate the following possible settings for an X Libris book:

Roman/Medieval/Barbarian
Ellizabethan/Renaissance/Restoration
Victorian/Edwardian
The Jazz Age (1920s & 30s)
Present day
Future
Other

B) Using the same scale of 1 to 5, please rate the following sexual possibilities for an X Libris book:

Submissive male/dominant female
Submissive female/dominant male
Lesbian sex
Gay male sex
Bondage/fetishism
Romantic love
Experimental sex (for example, anal/watersports/sex toys)
Group sex

C) Using the same scale of 1 to 5, please rate the following writing styles you might find in an X Libris book:

Realistic, down to earth, a true-to-life situation
Fantasy, escapist, but just possible
Completely unreal, out of bounds, dreamlike

248

D) From whose viewpoint would you prefer your ideal X Libris book to be written?

Main male characters
Main female characters
Both

E) What would your ideal X Libris heroine be like?

Dominant	Shy
Extroverted	Glamorous
Independent	Bisexual
Adventurous	Naïve
Intellectual	Kinky
Professional	Introverted
Successful	Ordinary
Other	

F) What would your ideal X Libris hero be like?

Caring	Athletic
Cruel	Sophisticated
Debonair	Retiring
Naïve	Outdoors type
Intellectual	Rugged
Professional	Kinky
Romantic	Hunky
Successful	Effeminate
Ordinary	Executive type
Sexually dominant	Sexually submissive
Other	

G) Is there one particular setting or subject matter that your ideal X Libris book would contain?

H) Please feel free to tell us about anything else you like/dislike about X Libris if we haven't asked you.

Thank you for taking time to tell us what you think about X Libris. Please tear this questionnaire out of the book now and post it back to us:

X Libris
Brettenham House
Lancaster Place
London WC2E 7EN

Other bestselling X Libris titles available by mail: